P9-EMH-296

Praise for SONGS FOR THE DEAF

Songs for the Deaf is a joyful, deranged, endlessly surprising book of stories that defy easy categorization, in addition to the laws of physics (girls "ride air," aliens plummet from the sky, a basketball-messiah shoots hoops). Fleming's prose is glorious music; his rhythms will get into your bloodstream, and his images will sink into your dreams. Thank you, Burrow Press, for bringing John Fleming's radioactively imaginative stories to us.

~Karen Russell, author of *Swamplandia!* and *Vampires in the Lemon Grove*

The range of characters and their concerns is matched by the tonal range, which shifts with aplomb from a certain canny comic zing to simple old sincerity. These stories somehow stay firmly on their tracks through wonderful narrative hairpin turns, the sentences sure in their gait, the language neither timid nor showy, and as with most satisfying stories, it's hard to tell whether the characters have guided themselves to the serendipitous endings they find, or whether they've been secretly dragged there by the superb skill of the storyteller.

~John Brandon, author of *A Million Heavens* and *Citrus County*

All music worth playing is worth playing loud, and the volume on *Songs for the Deaf* should be turned all the way up. John Henry Fleming riffs on renegade cloud readers, drifters seeking out their long-lost midwives, and random floating girls. In one sublime lick he intones a high-school basketball game as the Lord's Prayer. I've long admired his work, and this new collection—perfectly in touch with our fantastic times—is well worth blowing out a speaker or two.

~Jeff Parker, author of *Ovenman* and *The Taste of Penny*

DISCARD

JUN 02 2014

SONGS FOR THE DEAF

stories

JOHN HENRY FLEMING

PAPERBACK  ORIGINALS

Copyright © 2014 by John Henry Fleming

All Rights Reserved.

Paperback ISBN: 978-0-9849538-5-1

E-ISBN: 978-0-9849538-6-8

Book Design: Tina Holmes Craig

Cover Art: Lesley Silvia

Author Photo: Lacie Meier

First Edition. Published by Burrow Press, 2014

Print: burrowpress.com

Web: burrowpressreview.com

Flesh: functionallyliterate.org

Distributed by Itasca Books

5120 Cedar Lake Rd.

Minneapolis, MN 55416

orders@itascabooks.com

The following stories originally appeared, in slightly different versions, in the following magazines and anthologies: "Xenophilia" and "Weighing of the Heart" in *The North American Review*; "A Charmed Life" in *Better: Culture and Lit*; "Cloud Reader" in *Fourteen Hills*; "In the Shadow of the World's Greatest Monument to Love" in *Juked*; "Coward" in *Carve Magazine*; "Song for the Deaf" and "Revolutions" in *Atticus Review*; "The Day of Our Lord's Triumph (with marginal notes for children)" in *Kugelmass*; "The General" in *McSweeney's*; "The Posse" in *Mississippi Review*; and "Wind and Rain" in *Georgetown Review* and *100% Pure*

ACC LIBRARY SERVICES AUSTIN, TX

for Julie, Hayley, and Ethan

TABLE *of* CONTENTS

Cloud Reader

Return visits are easiest at night. In a dark suit and high, stiff collar, he knocks softly on back doors and waits there like a grim windbreak. Sometimes, as now, they expect him. They sent a messenger out to his campsite shortly after he arrived. An urgent matter involving their daughter, and double his usual fee.

A nervous, withered woman opens the back door for him and leads him down the hall into the small parlor, where the father stands with fists stuffed deep in his pockets. The man neither greets him nor invites him to take a seat. He simply asks him to place a hand on the girl's belly.

Curled into a chair, the girl brings her knees up and squeaks through pressed lips.

He's not a bad man, the mother tells her as she coaxes her up.

Last year, he remembers, a brilliant after-snow nimbus revealed a suitable match for the girl in question. A boy with family money, and the father approved. Now, with the girl still two years shy of legal marriage, the family's urgency can mean only one thing. He doesn't need clouds to understand that.

She's barely showing, offers the father. She's got a tight women's underthing to keep it in.

Will you be needing her to take that off? asks the mother.

He shakes his head. She's brought to him, a child and not a child, with a tiny growing secret in her belly. The curls fall away from her small neck, and her shoulders shake in her mother's arms. Behind a gloss of fear, her stare holds a frank strain of kindness, an understanding her parents lack. His own pain lets him see that more clearly.

To please the father, he places his unsteady fingertips on the pleated lavender cotton of her bodice and feels the stiff tight corset beneath.

A tiny thing encased. A growing shame. And it kicks.

He quickly withdraws his hand. This is beyond my talents, he tells them. I'm only a reader of clouds.

Tell us *something*! the father demands. We've paid once, and we'll pay you again. Tell us the sex of it!

He remembers disliking the father. A small-town banker accustomed to the sway of money. The fact that the last reading met his approval only confirmed that he'd put his money in the right place. Now this, and the man's sure he can buy his way out of it.

The girl sobs. Her pale brown ringlets coil and uncoil against her mother's cheek, while the corset forces out her breath in sharp little gasps.

He feels the girl's sense of loss. It occurs to him that if he'd followed another path he might now have a companion like her—daughter, wife, friend. Someone to know him, to keep him company on the rutted roads between towns. Someone to bear witness when he passes.

What does it matter now? Knowing what might have been is a skill of little value.

He agrees to one reading. For the daughter's sake.

Pleased he's gotten his way, the father retreats to the kitchen and returns with all the cloud reader has asked and more.

He refuses the extra. There's a limit to what he can do, and the fee he's asked is enough to press him uncomfortably against it.

Amen, says the mother.

•

That night, the wet breath of the plains grasses lifts out of the fields and descends on the town. Its citizens awake to thick gray blankets hanging heavy on the windows, the sunlight all but blocked. Neighbors haunt the streets. The known world diminished overnight, the encroaching mysteries a sudden reminder of the folly of knowing. Nothing, it seems, will ever be certain again.

The townspeople who cannot talk down the mystery look elsewhere for reassurance. Some stay inside. Others go to the preacher. Some inevitably connect the fog with the cloud reader's arrival, and the braver of those come to him. In a copse of musclewood between a fallow field and a creek, he's made a lean-to and a fire pit and strung a line to dry his clothes.

His visitors have ailments of body, mind, and soul. Some no more than insatiable curiosity. They want to know the curvature of their lives, and the angle of their demise, and if there's a design, can it not be reworked in their hands?

He makes no promises. They need only look at the senseless gray obscurity to understand what he's up against. The world has unlimited powers to conceal and confuse. When the time comes, he can only report what he sees. Meanwhile, he takes deposits, knowing that many will want them back when the fog clears and the need to know becomes less pressing.

As one day grays into the next, the slow-circling fog steps

cautiously through the denuded limbs of late November. It rises and falls, brightens and darkens, a living thing. He tries to accept its presence as a reminder of his limits.

•

When the preacher comes, crackling through the hazy field and into the trees, he wears a black suit and hat. Here's a switch, says the cloud reader, still in his long white underclothes. He's seen the preacher on both of his previous visits, but they've never spoken till now. Nothing good can come of it. Preachers fight an airy turf war but aren't so squeamish around muck. They spread rumors about the cloud reader's upbringing and habits. They incite their congregations.

He invites the preacher to sit against a tree while he pours him some of the coffee he's just brewed. The man has a robust torso and thin limbs; if he's going to do God's work, he'll have to do it with his stomach. He lowers himself with a groan and a thick exhale. When he removes his hat, he rubs his hand over his thinning black hair.

He says, You're going to be blamed for this, you know.

Fog's good for business, the cloud reader admits. The blame I'm used to.

I mean the boy. The father of the child.

When the cloud reader doesn't understand, the preacher makes a sound through his nose as he sips his coffee. The steam of it sweeps over his cheeks. Of course, says the preacher. Without the clouds you'd never know. He's dead.

The cloud reader shuts his eyes and sees the limits of his talent. He ought to have expected it.

Hanged himself last night, the preacher says. I've come from the funeral just now.

He senses the man's satisfaction in delivering this news

and remembers how much he dislikes preachers. In Ames last month there was a man who tried to trick him into helping him with a sale. When the deal fell through, the man complained to his preacher how cloud readers were bad for public morality. A public beating was arranged to prove it. And now this. A boy is dead; there will have to be a reason.

Are you any less to blame? he asks the preacher.

The man claws and releases his coffee cup on the ground beside him, one knee raised, black vest unbuttoned. Blasphemy won't help your case, if it comes to that.

And you'll let it, I suppose.

The preacher says nothing. He doesn't have to.

•

He walks through the bleak obscurity miles beyond the town limits, beyond any hope of an accurate reading, just to comprehend the extent of the gloom. He finds weaknesses in its structure, coincidental separations of its layers glimmering with hope of sunlight. Then nothing. To look up and be denied even a shape! Sometimes the incommunicability of the world rankles him.

He made a promise to the girl's family—to the girl, in whose eyes he saw what might have been. He'll wait for the fog to lift, though he understands what it might cost him. A boy has died. The wound of it will have to be closed.

He feels his way into town in the black, moonless night, his footsteps cough in the quiet, the pain in his chest shortening his breath. The pain took hold these last few months, and now it grows by the day, a deep pit that swallows life's convictions. Its searing advances peel back nerves till his hands shake. He knows he doesn't have much longer before it takes him. He's not even sure he'll have the strength to turn his eyes to the clouds when the fog finally clears. And if he dies here, he'll give the preacher the satisfaction of another Christian burial.

A lamp still burns at the house. The parents are waiting for him, and the maid lets him in.

She's feeling poorly, the mother says. We've sent her on to bed.

Does she know? the cloud reader asks them. About the boy?

The father stands by the kitchen door, his jaw set and his eyes to the floor. The woman looks to her husband before answering.

We thought it best not to trouble her. In her condition.

I wish you'd been more careful, says the father. The whole town knows you're here.

I don't avoid it, he says. I have a living to earn.

Didn't I pay you enough? You could have kept to yourself out by the creek. Now the boy's dead and they're asking questions.

The floorboards above them creak and the mother puts her nervous fingers to her lips. She'll hear.

She's bound to soon enough, the father says, folding and unfolding his arms. Tell us something! We've paid for it! Tell us the thing's sex! If you can read clouds, you can read bellies.

What difference does it make?

My wife's gone barren and I don't have a boy of my own, the man says. He stares at his wife as he would a broken tool. I could send the girl and her mother off to her aunt's in Minnesota for the winter.

And if it's not a boy?

There's something can be done. I've already been to Ames and asked about it.

The mother puts her face in her hands and has trouble catching her breath. The father stretches his neck.

The stupidity of someone like him deciding her fate, he thinks; there will never be an answer for that.

When the woman breaks into sobs, the father grows furious. Stop this, he tells her. You have only yourself to blame. I knew you were a fake, he says to the cloud reader. A wives' tale. It was her idea to let you in the first time, and now look! None of this would have happened. If you can't undo what you've done, I'll find someone who will.

I made a promise and I'll do the reading, he says. But not for your sake.

A tremor rattles the length of his arm. His chest burns. The cloud reader pulls their money out of his pocket and sets it on the desk under the stairs. It's no good to him anyway.

•

What will he do when the fog clears and the clouds have more to say than he cares to know? If the clouds tell him the sex, will he listen? If they tell him the unborn is a girl, will he speak the truth? He's always believed that his service is to see plainly and disclose all. The moment he intercedes, his talents are compromised, and he can no longer trust himself. If he lies to the father, who's to say he hasn't lied to himself? The conviction he's built his profession on will fall into doubt, his life's work reduced to a showman's sham. And yet he cannot let himself be responsible for the death of the unborn child.

The fog has begun to thin, and he walks through flashes of lightly filtered sunlight painful to his unaccustomed eyes. He avoids looking up, afraid what he might see.

At night he keeps a small fire burning and sits with his back against a tree, absorbing its mute glow. Behind him, the creek gurgles under black skies. Currents of cool damp air finger through the fire's dry heat and sweep across his skin like rags. He thinks about the boy. About the world the boy imagined where the birth of a child is worse than death. As he climbed the tree with his rope, what did he feel? Did he think of the kind-eyed girl? Of the child he'd never have, the small face of the future he wouldn't see? He leapt into an abyss with blind faith in his rope—to stop his fall, to lift him into open skies. What answer could he have hoped for in that infinite muteness?

The cloud reader might have dozed. The fire has grown quiet. Then he hears noises with bobbing lights attached. They come through the field and stop under the trees, just beyond the dim firelight. A scouting party in the battle of doubt. They don't have a clear leader, and each seems to wait for the others to talk. Their lamps light chins and noses and ribbons of light in their deep-set eyes.

A community request? he asks.

One clears his throat. No request in it. Either leave on your own or come with us.

He thinks he recognizes the speaker. The man had stood over by the tree one day while his wife sought a reading concerning the health of their twin boys. She brought the cloud reader half a cake as payment. Perhaps he spoke first for fear the cloud reader would bring this up.

He wouldn't. Contradictions of faith and deed are the foundation of his profession, his bread and butter. And unlike the preacher, he doesn't have a thick book to defend himself. He has only the clouds, who have yet to break a man's fall.

I made a promise, he says. I intend to keep it.

Promises from swindlers don't stand up, says one.

You preach lies, says another.

They bind his hands and push him through the darkness

to the city jail, where a deputy stands waiting. They charge him with threatening public morality and disturbing the peace because they can't legally charge him with making fog or doubt.

I don't preach anything, the cloud reader says.

·

At night, in the blackness, nothing seems changed except his sleeping arrangements—colder than his campsite, the thin mattress less comfortable than a blanket folded beneath him. He isn't used to sleeping indoors, and the thick walls seem false in their silence.

Before the sun grays the sky out his barred window, the room is lit and the preacher let in. He still wears his black suit.

The cloud reader leans up on an elbow. You dressing for me this time?

The deputy shuts the bars and the preacher grips the bench as he eases onto it. The silver buttons of his vest catch the lamplight. When he leans forward, his thighs cradle the hang of his wide belly, a grotesque pregnancy that will never reach term.

The law will run its course, the preacher assures him.

Looks to me a verdict's been reached.

These are well-meaning people. They find their own ways to do what's right. You ought to have left, but at least you're safe. Things could have been worse.

The cloud reader laughs. I'd like to see a copy of your Sunday sermon.

I know the girl's father, says the preacher. There's one thing you can do to save yourself and the child.

I won't do it.

Do you know the kind of man he's spoken to in Ames? Do you know what he'll do to the girl and her child? The father's not a man comfortable in doubt.

A community trait, I've noticed. But I suppose it keeps us both employed.

Blasphemy again.

He's got a plan to send the wife and daughter away, says the cloud reader. He could do that no matter the sex.

The risk is too great. People already suspect the truth. To him, only a son would justify the trouble. People will recognize that, and they'll accept the lie in the interest of filling a void. You know how these towns work.

Too well, I'm afraid.

If you keep silent, he'll choose the sure thing. Just to be rid of the trouble. But if you could tell him something. Tell him it's a boy. You'd be preventing a mortal sin.

The cloud reader looks out the window. It's as if the world has grown old and its eyesight dimmed. Look for yourself, he says. There's nothing to say.

Just say what he wants to hear. All of this mess would clear up and you'd be on your way unmolested. I'd see to it.

Why don't *you* tell him?

I'm afraid, in a matter like this, it's you he'd trust.

The cloud reader laughs to hear it. What a thing for a preacher to admit! It makes him more kindly disposed. But of course he can't do it. Not to save himself some trouble; not even to save a life.

The preacher is pulling on one sideburn, and the cloud reader can see he has a struggle of his own. His prayers have failed. His sermons have failed. The pages of his book, with row upon row of crisp black signs, hold no more certainty for him than the billows and blurred margins of clouds.

The cloud reader says nothing more. He lies back on

his cot with his hands behind his head and stares out the barred window. The fog has a flickering quality, the sunlight discovering its weaknesses. While it swirled before, now the fluttering curtains of it travel slowly in one direction. Perhaps that means it will soon clear up. Perhaps it means nothing.

The preacher stares at the floor for several minutes, then draws his feet in and stands. He motions for the deputy to let him out.

•

That night the air grows colder and the fog moves into his cell, into his breath. Only his chest is warm with pain, something digging its nails into his lungs, announcing its claim with a seductive whisper—that nothing matters now, that nothing ever has. Even the strength of his convictions will soon fall into that growing blackness in his chest. And then he'll have resisted for nothing.

He shivers from time to time, but the mattress has grown more comfortable, the silence less stable. There are moments when he thinks he sees pinpricks of light through his bars. He blinks and they're gone. Did he only imagine the breathy shush of the fog, its bodiless stream changing course?

Out of it at last grows a sound more distinct, edges forming as it moves closer. Halting steps. A pause. The whisper of clothes. Her form a single shade blacker than night.

He stands up, thankful for the small release of energy, and steps to the window. When the darkness falters, he sees the layers of clothes, the shawl. The slight lift of her belly, released from its corset. She sets a bag down at her feet and raises her chin to the window.

It's as if she's understood everything; if he can't continue, she'll walk his steps for him, a companion after the fact. Isn't that the next best thing?

You're a brave girl, he tells her. But you shouldn't delay. There'll be light soon.

I'm giving thanks where it's due, she says, her clear voice a chime in the fog.

I've done nothing, he says.

Sometimes isn't that enough?

He smiles in the darkness. He's been right about her all along. She saw him and knew; she's different from the rest. Where will you go? he asks her.

I have an aunt in Minnesota. By the time my father finds out, it will be too late.

It's far, he says. You may not make it before the snow.

I'll take my chances. She draws a deep breath and rests one hand on her belly. She reaches for her bag but changes her mind. Will you tell me… she begins. What do you see in the clouds that others don't?

A child's question. He's never been asked it. The others only want answers to their needs and are too frightened or distracted to know more.

We all have our paths to conviction, he says, and lets it go at that.

At least now I know which way to go, she says.

He nods, though she might not have seen it.

If he'd followed another track, if the whims of his decisions had turned his eyes to earth like the rest of humanity, she would not be traveling alone. Knowing it is enough. He can take solace now in the possibilities of the past, a thousand unlived lives in a bag drawn tight at the top. His life is more than the one he's lived.

He reaches into his pocket and takes the last of the money

he received from the townspeople. You'll need this, he says.

She accepts it in her small, gloved fingers. Thank you again, she says, and she picks up her own bag to leave.

He puts one hand on the iron bar, wet from their breath, and looks for her kind eyes in the darkness.

Here's the answer to his pain's bleak seduction. His life has mattered all along, in more ways than he has let himself know. And it matters now as she carries it away.

•

The children seem to know first. They approach his barred window through the thinning fog, call him names and run. Some throw clumps of icy clay that shatter against the bars and spray into his cell. He's tired now and doesn't bother to move from his bed or to brush the dirt from his face or clothes. He shuts his eyes but can't sleep. It's grown colder with daybreak, and it takes some concentration not to shiver. Then he hears men's voices gathering in the street. He tries not to discern the words but instead to concentrate on the sound as if it's a building wind. And it does build. It gains force and direction until the impediments mean nothing. It won't be long now. The deputy in the next room understands; the cloud reader can hear him pacing. Pausing and pacing. At last the deputy opens a door and leaves.

The wind diminishes and the street quiets. And then the sound builds rapidly until the door bursts open again. He keeps his eyes closed and listens while they find the key. The cell door opens. They're cursing him. The pain in his chest seems to rot him from inside. He keeps his mind on the wind. Ages seem to pass before they lay hands on his arms and yank him up. Pairs of hands grip him tightly on each side, and another hand claws his shirt between the shoulder blades and twists, exposing his lower back to the frigid air.

What are they yelling? He tries now to understand, to pick out a word or two that might anchor him. He can't. His senses have dulled. The sounds are warm mists on his cheeks and neck. Outside, the fog's wet motes glow like a billion miniature crystals collecting the faint light. And they move; a space is opening for him.

Clumps of people brave the cold and gather outside shops and houses as he passes, their steaming faces little concentrations of warmth, losing themselves breath by breath. The men pushing him along wheeze as if they've run a great distance. Do any of them struggle with what they're about to do? Is his public walk part of their own path to conviction? He knows how doubts are resolved in small increments. Can you find a way to take a man from his cell? Can you find a way to lead him through town? To put a rope around his neck? And once you've done that, the last step is easy. It has the force of pattern behind it, a swirling wind gathering strength and direction. The paths to conviction are always circular.

They pass the church, a small but impressive structure with a steeple rising two stories above the sanctuary and two small panels of stained glass in the heavy doors. Only those colored panels show any signs of light.

Beyond the last building, his escorts angle him through a field to the base of an oak tree. A man with a noose stands waiting. The cloud reader's wrists are yanked together and tied. He raises his head and assesses the thinning fog, breaking now into soft-edged shapes with faint traces of blue. Even if there's time, will he still have the strength to see?

He knows his gift is a fragile blessing, a thing he grasped only in the months long ago after his mother died and his father left. He was fourteen and alone then; the farm was failing. He went out to the field day after day intending to plow, to plant, and day after day he lay in the dirt and weeds and stared into the clouds. Not looking for answers at first. Just staring. Until he began to recognize patterns, familiar shapes and motions. He admired the way they built themselves, seemingly out of nothing, clawing up to overtake the sun. Others like pale daggers thrown at the horizon. Or black banks of night's angry castoffs, rumbling and spitting over the land. Their smooth skin would boil on hot days, their edges fade as it cooled. They marched together. Or overrode each other at surprising angles. They shrank before his eyes, vanished and reappeared. It all had to mean something, didn't it?

The thought made him laugh, there on the dirt on his family's dying farm. Of course it didn't have to mean anything. But why couldn't it? The thin high clouds, cold and faceless, depressed him. The low white puffs gave him hope. There was a connection. Wasn't that enough?

Of course not. But what else was? His father had awoken each day long before sunrise and read from his Bible, and when he left, the thick black book was the one thing he took with him, the thing that mattered more than his son.

He remembered his father in the days after his mother's death, reading the book day and night, flipping the thin pages, searching for something in the crisp black signs. What had he found? What path through those pages led him to leave his only child and his farm and walk away in the middle of the night? The strength of that conviction was a thing to admire.

The son would find his own conviction in clouds. He stared harder. It was a joke and not a joke, like everything else he could think of. And then one day the weather turned cold and it was too late to plow and plant and there was no reason to stay. He followed the dried ruts for days until a man on a wagon stopped him just outside a small town. The man had been looking for a farmhand; did the boy know his farming? No. He was thinking of building a new barn; did the boy know building? *No.* Well, was he a hard worker and quick learner, at least? *Not especially.* Won't be easy for a boy like that to make his way in this world; did he have any kind of useful skill at all? *Yes. I'm a reader of clouds.*

The man laughed. He shook his horse's reins and the horse carried him away, still laughing. The boy went on into town, and when he found no business, he went on to the next, and the next, until the sheer strength of his conviction caused someone to want to know. A tiny scrap of certainty, he learned, was a valuable commodity in an uncertain world. And also a threat.

Beside the oak's thick trunk, his head is dipped into the noose. The rough hemp scratches at his Adam's apple. They're quieter now. They don't need the yelling to convince themselves anymore.

He's led to a ladder and forced up its steps. Two pairs of hands steady him while the other end of the rope is thrown over a thick branch above.

He waits. The rope is pulled tight, and he has trouble swallowing. He can hear them breathing.

A patch of warmth at the top of his head makes him open his eyes and look. The fog has split, and the sky opens above it. It's the first blue he's seen in weeks. And there, moving through his narrow line of sight, is a small white cloud, smooth-skinned and frayed at the edge.

It's a girl, he thinks.

A Charmed Life

His father was a disgraced steamboat pilot with a knack for grounding boats and destroying docks, his mother the thin-lipped illegitimate daughter of a beefy prostitute. When the midwife handed him over, she waited six hours in the parlor room to be paid, her queries up the decrepit stairs returned only by the newborn's trembling squalls. Decades later, old and infirm, she still made the joke she had the rights to him. By then, no one remembered who she was talking about.

The town never gave him a chance. His father's reputation would prevent him from getting decent work; his mother's would prevent him from associating with quality families or courting a decent girl. Broke and restless, he left home at sixteen.

He took an interest in banjo and hoped to make a living in St. Louis, picking old tunes for bar crowds. But the saloons there weren't interested in hick banjo players or sentimental hick songs. They preferred half-naked women who could blow a flute while jiggling their breasts—skills he didn't have.

He rode a train westward, having heard of fortunes made in San Francisco, but his train got held up outside Ellsworth, Kansas, and he was taken hostage by a band of cutthroats some say was the James Gang. Pleased with their take, the gang's leader offered him a hundred bucks for his troubles. When he declined, knowing the worth of a thing tainted, the gang leader shot him in the foot for his ingratitude.

The story of his capture made him a hero in Ellsworth. A judge up for re-election offered him a clerk's position, saying that a young man with his kind of experience was worth a hundred Harvard grads. He took the job, intending to resume his journey to San Francisco as soon as his foot healed. The foot was treated by a doctor with a reputation for cutting corners to get back to his drinking; the procedure left him with a permanent limp.

The judge won his first re-election but lost the next, and then it turned out that a man worth a hundred Harvard grads was not even employable to clean livery stalls. He hopped aboard the same westbound train that had once been held up outside Ellsworth. This time the train was held up outside Reno. One of the robbers had been a member of the gang who'd taken him hostage previously. This man recognized him and took him hostage again, for old times' sake.

That night, sitting beside a campfire, he made the mistake of telling his captors his life story so far, including the few years he'd spent clerking for the judge in Ellsworth. He'd had some setbacks, he said, but now he was sure he'd find his worth in this world. One of the gang members—a different one—had had a brother sentenced to death by that judge in Ellsworth. The robbers took a vote and decided to kill their hostage. It was clear from his story that they'd get no money anyway if they held him for ransom. They threw a rope over a tree limb, slipped a noose around his neck, and declared themselves agents of divine retribution.

As it turned out, their drinking skills were much better

than their engineering skills. When a couple of them tried to yank him up from the ground, he bent one knee, gagged a bit, and before long had them convinced he was dead. When they released the rope, he let himself go limp and crumple to the dirt. As soon as they returned to the campfire, he stood up in the darkness and left. Who knows what the gang thought the next morning? They were all killed in a shoot-out with the feds.

As he walked across the Nevada desert rubbing his rope-burnt neck, San Francisco seemed the answer to all his worldly wants. There'd be fresh drinking water. Food, too. And when he'd had his fill of those, there'd be women, whom he'd very much like to know better.

For several months he wandered generally westward and up into the mountains, occasionally circling back when delirium overcame him. He survived on rodents, hunting at dusk and using his quick feet to step on their tails. His beard grew long, his clothes tattered. His lips swelled and cracked, and dried animal blood spotted his cheeks and nose. This is the condition in which a young widow discovered him one October morning, some six months after the night her husband disappeared and three months after she'd begun calling herself a young widow.

She found this hairy apparition a fine example of the American Yeti, whom she'd taken to studying in her widowhood. She called it "studying" in her head, but since there were no books on the fabled creature—at least none available to a lone woman in a remote sierra cabin—the studying amounted to hours of thinking—about his appearance, his origins, his eating habits, his mating habits. The latter she'd taken an especial interest in, as flashes of exotic, musty couplings warmed her lonesome hours. The fantasy Other, as she came to think of him, grew hairier and dirtier and less verbal in her thoughts, and when his big, rough hands grabbed her naked hips in dreams, their animal grunts filled her starry nights in chorus.

So when the stranger walked out of the trees that cool afternoon, naked, stooped, grunting, she did not reach for her gun. She tore open her dress instead.

At first, she found it merely curious that he could talk; this fact forced her to re-examine her Yeti thought-studies. Then other little things began to bother her, like when she cleaned him up in the cold mountain stream he didn't look nearly so bestial—only pale and undernourished. When she tried to discourage him from bathing he did it himself anyway, which made his skin almost womanly smooth and his scent almost floral. And when in the glade she displayed her rump for mating in Yeti fashion, he told her, with disturbing intelligibility, that he preferred the bed in the cabin, and wouldn't she, too, like to get cleaned up a little?

Her zealous embrace of brutehood had yanked him back to his own neglected humanity. He awoke as if from a dream, remembering his visions of San Francisco and the journey that lay ahead. He told her he was sorry, that it was his fault he'd lost his taste for raw meat and open-air sexual commerce.

Then what the hell good are you? she wanted to know.

He didn't know how to respond. When he left, she set fire to the cabin and roamed the woods naked, preying on small beasts and hunting for a less adulterated specimen of her fantasy Other. One night, she stalked and attacked several pioneer families. Mistaken for a wildcat, she was shot and killed.

His yearning for San Francisco again pulled him westward. High in the sierras, having yet to stumble upon a wagon trail or footpath, he trekked over sharp terrain. He developed a set of climbing skills that would one day be the envy of freestyle mountaineers everywhere and he began, at the top of each mountain, to challenge himself to climb the tallest peak in sight. In this manner, he zigzagged through the mountains, almost certainly becoming the first man to climb all the high peaks in California in his thickly calloused bare feet.

There were sightings. Other travelers would look up from the dusty wagon trail and spy a distant, man-shaped figure high on a snowy peak. Two competing superstitions arose among the pioneers: for some, his appearance meant easy times; for others, hard. The easy-timers saw him and forged ahead even against bad weather. The hard-timers turned back and wintered in Reno, or else gave up their journeys altogether. Prayed to and cursed, unaware of his growing status down below, he climbed onward until at last the mountains gave up and he descended into a rich, golden valley.

Upon closer inspection, the valley looked to be covered in dead grass. What sort of disaster had befallen California? Had this plague, stretching as far as the eye could see in three directions and contained only by the high mountains at his back, propagated outward from his beloved San Francisco? Had one of the huge sailing ships laden with worldly riches also contained a pestilential stowaway with an appetite for American greenery? He stopped at the edge of the field and listened for the hum of locusts. He sniffed for foul air. When a handful of magpies appeared and descended upon an unseen carcass in the grass, he took it as a sign and turned around, intent on warning travelers of the awful calamity.

His joints began to ache. His youth seemed behind him.

He came upon a two-track trail and followed it east until he met up with a pair of wagons. The wagons carried a Mormon family hoping to settle in California. The patriarch, Hosea Loblolly, explained over a cup of warm coffee that they'd been harassed by feds in Utah who'd begun arresting polygamists. There'd been shots exchanged, and one of Hosea's wives had been mortally wounded. She'd died en route. Would he like to view her?

He followed Hosea around to the back of the second wagon. Hosea swished a mouthful of coffee and spat it out, as if to cleanse his tongue. He pulled open the curtains to reveal a girl of not more than thirteen, her chin turned down and to the side, the saddest expression he'd ever seen stamped indelibly onto her face. Her skin had darkened and she'd begun to decompose in the heat. Though the smell was nearly unbearable, neither said anything. Hosea waved the flies off her.

"I aimed to raise her up with my good deeds," said Hosea. "She died too soon. Now I feel the responsibility to bear her mortal remains until I've redeemed us both with an act of grace. May her soul rest in everlasting peace on the right side of God." Both turned away.

The face of the girl had nearly erased the sight of the long, dead valley. "I've seen something," he said, remembering. He told Hosea about the shocking plague that had murdered California, including, he assumed, the golden city of San Francisco. He encouraged Hosea to turn back before the plague found its way into the mountains and killed them too.

Hosea stared at him a long moment before turning his eyes westward at the mountains. He chewed repeatedly on his bottom lip like he was trying to roll it into a cigarette. "Well," he said, "there'd be some grace to it."

Hosea shook his hand, reloaded his family in one wagon,

climbed into the driver's seat of the other—the one with the dead girl—and resumed his westward journey.

The dead girl's face would stick with him as fare for the journey he'd never take.

Back in Reno, he wanted more than anything to rest in a woman's arms, and the women at the Dalton Ranch were happy to oblige—until they discovered he had no money. Johnny Dalton, whose privates had long ago been crushed by a cuckolded brickmaker, kept the ranch running primarily for the opportunities afforded him by occasions like this. He and a pair of assistants pummeled the penniless john to the threshold of death. Then they let him recover in the back room until he was ready for another pummeling. When they finally left him face down in the street, a cart rolled over his already broken legs.

Having set aside a little money after skimming Johnny's profits, Nessie Torino, one of the older women at the Dalton, took the opportunity to retire and nurse the beaten john back to health, seeing in him a glimmer of hope beyond the rigid transactional constraints of her professional life. She rented a couple of clean rooms above the post office and attended his needs for several months. He didn't walk well after his beating, and his face was permanently scarred and asymmetrical due to the broken cheek. He whistled when he breathed. The upside was that his old gunshot limp didn't matter so much anymore.

She supported them both for a time, having landed a position sorting mail at the post office below, whose postmaster had been a regular client for years. When Johnny Dalton got wind of it, he accused her of disloyalty and threatened the postmaster and anyone else who hired her. The postmaster reasoned that the town was not generous enough to suffer two men who whistled with each breath. He had a connection in San Francisco where, he told Nessie, they were more open-minded about professional women.

Up in their rooms, she resorted to all her professional tricks to try to convince him to come along. He considered her offer. He considered it some more.

But every time he re-imagined the journey (tougher now, with his broken body), he stopped short at the dead valley. No, he didn't think he could walk across that, even though both Nessie and the postmaster assured him the valley had greened up again, as it did each spring, and San Francisco was never better. But he couldn't imagine it. Even if they reached San Francisco, the city would be different now. In his thoughts, at least, its golden days were past.

She cried when she left, and he did too, once she was out of sight.

He took her job at the post office, which for some reason insulted Johnny Dalton much less. After a few months, he'd saved enough for a ticket back to Ellsworth, where he'd once felt comfortable and well-liked.

When he arrived, no one remembered him, and he was too modest to recount his escape many years ago from the cutthroat gang of train robbers, which had faded from popular memory in any case. He had no desirable physical skills now that his body was broken, and what he'd learned in his years with the judge was now either forgotten or obsolete.

He hopped a freight car bound for St. Louis.

There he found a nostalgic wave had swept the saloons, owing to a recent cholera outbreak. All the old tunes he used to play on the banjo as a young man could be heard up and down the riverfront each night.

His broken appearance and especially his whistling breath earned him enough sympathy to panhandle change for a beat-up banjo. By the time he approached bar owners for an audition, the nostalgia wave had passed in all but the seediest establishments. One of those establishments offered him a three-night-a-week gig in exchange for two bits and two free beers.

He hadn't considered that his hands had aged along with the rest of him. They tired quickly, and he had to take a rest every twenty minutes. This irked the bar owner, who threatened him with firing and then with bodily harm. Knowing he wouldn't last long, he began selling his beers half-price to the other customers, and he was able, before he was finally discovered and shoved into the street with a broken banjo, to save up a small reserve which he thought of, with a newfound sense of irony, as his nest egg. The ironic thought led to an earnest plan, and he decided after all these years to return to his hometown.

He didn't want to spend his money on a boat ticket, and there were no trains running between St. Louis and his town, so he walked. For the first three days, he wasn't sure he'd make it. His legs were so tired, and movement so painful, he rested more often than not. His labored, whistling breaths raised flocks of geese a hundred yards through the trees. Tired and numb, he worked himself into a slow, stumbling rhythm and arrived in town a walking corpse.

He'd assumed his parents were dead, and he was right. He'd also assumed, and was right, that his siblings, like himself, had scattered away to escape the family reputation. So why had he returned? There was a woman he wanted to check on. He stood before her tiny house at the far end of town, away from the river. He wasn't sure if she'd still remember him, or if she still lived in this same house, or if she was even alive, but if he waited much longer he'd never make it up to her door.

He knocked, and it took her five minutes to shuffle over and pull the door open. They stood looking at each other. She was much smaller than he remembered. Her long black curtain of hair had thinned and blanched, her cheeks sagged like dough, and she smelled like household dust. Her pale lips had stretched to a small but permanent grin. And he could see in her clear dark eyes that she remembered him.

He took the last of his money out of his pocket and handed it to her, payment for her services long ago. He felt the little squall of relief that comes with having nothing.

The midwife counted the money twice and nodded, then lifted the corners of her lips just barely and in a high, thin whisper spoke the words he'd been waiting for. "I always said you'd amount to something."

The Day of Our Lord's Triumph

(with marginal notes for children)

After the Righteous End, Our Lord, The Survivor, walked out of the Devastation and told us His stories. We share them now to understand His Greatness and the Significance of His Life.

On this Day of His Earthly Triumph, Our Lord returned from His hours of schooling and served Himself a small platter of triangular chips. He ate the chips point-first, making mash of them and vanquishing their sharp-edged power to harm the tender insides of Our Lord's mouth and throat. He thereupon washed down the harmless mash with sparkling syrup and was pleased.

Just as we today take our Communion Chips from bags we find in the Heaps.

Having thus satisfied the ache in His belly, Our Lord moved His body to the sofa, and there sat upon its soft leather skin, for which the cattle did sacrifice their lives to increase Our Lord's comfort. Our Lord expelled the bubbling gasses from His stomach and placed His feet upon the coffee table, an act often persecuted by his worldly parents.

Thus do we honor the beasts of the field.

Yet Our Lord did persevere.

Amen!

Pressing His thumb to the buttons of the remote, Our Lord raised the television into being. He switched channels according to His whim, His

Today we sigh in prayerful quietude before the lightless screens on our altars, even as we await the return of the Lord's New Season, when our screens will shine again with His light and bring delight to all!

sovereign eyes scanning the myriad and tawdry offerings. Golden Calves paraded before His sight in the guise of False Gospel, yet Our Lord remained strong. Having judged these things harshly, He banished all light from the screen.

Our Lord discarded the remote and sighed.

He left the house, warmed by a light jacket He pulled from a hook beside the door. He slid His hands into the pockets of His jean shorts. The wind did blow His thick hair about His head and into His eyes, and He slouched against the chill gusts. He crossed the lawn and followed a concrete trail. He discovered in the pocket of His jacket the Nano He had been missing for two weeks, and He took this as a sign. When He tucked the earbuds into His ears and pressed the play button, the piano introduction to Jethro Tull's "Locomotive Breath" did illuminate His being.

Such are the strains we hear in the Sacrament of Holy Matrimony.

Our Lord bobbed His head at the power of the wailing guitar that followed. He achieved inner peace despite ample signs of worldly decadence—decapitated grass and geometric shrubs, trash cans aligned neatly at the curbs, mailboxes shining like the gaudy plumage of tropical birds—the signs of enslavement to a false order which He did reject, as He did also reject the order His worldly parents attempted to force upon His dwelling space. For this He was on several occasions unjustly imprisoned.

This is why our churches are open to the sky and we adorn our pews and aisles with offerings of unwashed clothes.

Our Lord knew the dangers of His journey

through the neighborhood. For all around Him dwelt His Sworn Enemies, and the Sworn Enemies did taunt Our Lord continually with epithets and condemnations. The Sworn Enemies did sometimes pour glue through the vents of His locker at school. They casually tripped Him in the hallways. They were clever in their ways, feigning clumsiness or momentary spasms that sent their feet and elbows flying into Our Lord's path and uttering their epithets beyond the hearing of authorities. Thus did they torment Our Lord with impunity.

Yet Our Lord did persevere.

Amen!

Now He traveled past the public ball courts, where several Sworn Enemies battled Newcomers in a game of 3-on-3. The Sworn Enemies, taking note of Our Lord's passage, did shout unholy oaths and challenges to His manhood, whereupon Our Lord raised His finger in retort.

Just as today we raise our fingers against all who challenge Our Lord's sovereignty.

The Sworn Enemies heeded not the warning of His finger. They swore to destroy Him as soon as they defeated the Three Newcomers.

Our Lord raised the volume of His Nano until the Jethro Tull playlist filled His ears.

Soon He came upon the Two Magenta-Haired Girls sitting outside the 7-Eleven, sipping cherry Slurpees through their painted lips. Our Lord was familiar with these girls and had reason to believe they were friendly to His ways, as they, too, had been unjustly labeled by the Sworn Enemies and by whose influence were cast out as harlots

We bob our heads each Sunday in spiritual agreement with the palpitations of St. Ian's flute and permit ourselves the joyful riffs of our air guitars, for we are created in His image.

and loose women, though Our Lord knew this to be false, having sought fleshly congress with both girls at a party and receiving for His efforts a bruise to His lip.

Amen!

Our Lord did persevere.

He removed one ear bud and nodded His head in greeting. The Magenta-Haired Girls slurped from their drinks.

One of the Magenta-Haired Girls had a new skateboard and Our Lord did ask if He could ride it.

The Magenta-Haired Girl who owned the skateboard asked if it were true that Our Lord did prefer boys to girls, as some of His Sworn Enemies claimed.

Our Lord denied it. Did they not remember the party last year where He had sought fleshly congress with them?

The Magenta-Haired Girls claimed they did not remember, and they doubted the truth of Our Lord's advances. He had not made an impression.

Amen!

Our Lord did persevere.

You may recognize these actions as the source of our Confirmation ceremony!

He said nothing of the bruise He did suffer at their hands. He climbed upon the skateboard and rode it skillfully across the uneven concrete and loose gravel in the parking lot, pumping to gain speed and avoiding a car backing from its space. The car honked at Our Lord and its owner did shout an oath.

The Magenta-Haired Girls were filled with mirth.

Our Lord swerved around a discarded can. He avoided collision with a small bird darting from a puddle. Our Lord performed well on the board until its turning radius proved larger than expected. The board struck a parking block and Our Lord stumbled forward and slammed against the window of the 7-Eleven.

Yet Our Lord did persevere.

Amen!

He quickly retrieved the board and returned it to the mirthful Girls, explaining to them that the board's trucks were in need of loosening.

The Magenta-Haired Girls appeared skeptical.

Feeling unesteemed, Our Lord reached a fateful decision. He informed The Magenta-Haired Girls that He was going to the basketball courts to defeat His enemies this very day, and would they like to witness it?

Is it any wonder we "Pass the Rock" in church? We celebrate Our Lord's game and fear His mad skills!

The Magenta-Haired Girls' faces expressed doubt.

Our Lord informed them that He had been working out in preparation for the battle.

The First Magenta-Haired Girl wanted to know if Our Lord had been working out at the same time He practiced his skateboard riding.

The Second Magenta-Haired Girl laughed.

Our Lord bid the Magenta-Haired Girls good-bye and passed through the doorway into the 7-Eleven, where the Clerk announced to Him that he would be watching his movements on the monitors.

Now you see the meaning of the magenta chalk used for decoration at the annual Festival of Doubt, as well as the reason it is scrubbed clean when the festival ends.

Our Lord approached the Clerk. He said, Friend, why do you accuse me? I have never taken from your store.

I don't know You, but I know Your type, the

Clerk replied.

And what type is that? Our Lord asked.

Punks Who Steal to Impress Their Slutty Girlfriends Because They Cannot Ride a Skateboard, said the Clerk.

When Our Lord disputed the truth of this, the Clerk did angrily order Him from the store, leaving Our Lord's thirst unslaked.

You bear false witness against Me! Our Lord shouted through the glass door as the Clerk locked it shut, though Our Lord did know that Justice would be rendered in due course.

For Our Lord did persevere.

The Magenta-Haired Girls were gone, and Our Lord did feel a growing impatience at the willful ignorance of Mankind. He understood that today He would have to make a stand against his Sworn Enemies and the ignorance of their kind. He had made His decision.

Thus did Our Lord return to the public courts.

The Sworn Enemies had just defeated the Three Newcomers there, and the six of them rested in the shade of a racquetball court's wall as Our Lord did unlatch the gate and step onto the asphalt.

The Two Magenta-Haired Girls had arrived before Him and stood now on the dirt beyond the backboard, speaking mirthfully into their phones, exhorting many to come witness Our Lord's certain defeat.

There He is, said the largest of the Sworn

We say today not to "clerk" one's neighbor or you will lock yourself in glass. We take heed at the lessons of Our Lord.

Amen!

These used to exist.

In such manner do we mock our Lord and his powers during the Festival of Doubt, only to renew our faith more strongly at its conclusion.

Enemies. Come to get a beat-down.

Our Lord bravely stepped forward and announced His intention to vanquish them.

The Sworn Enemies made jest of Him.

Our Lord turned to the Newcomers. Whosoever of you will join Me, rise now to your feet, for if you are not with Me, you are against Me, and you shall suffer the fate of My enemies.

One of them claimed to have stubbed his toe.

A stubbed toe is as nothing to the sufferings of Hell, Our Lord did point out.

The Boy with the Stubbed Toe chose unwisely. We speak of his sorrowful fate in our lessons.

The other two Newcomers rose to join Our Lord. One of them asked Our Lord if He had game.

You shall see, said Our Lord.

The Manifold Witnesses did now begin to gather at the courts. They came in singles and pairs and small groups. A cool wind did blow, and the Manifold Witnesses braced themselves against it. They wore long shorts and short shorts and low jeans and shirts with various sayings representing the many tribes. Some hung onto the fence and peered through it or over it. Some sat in the dirt. Some perched on the play structures. Some lined the court at their peril.

Unseasonable at the time, and a portent of the Cleansing Devastation that Our Lord did harness with His unparalleled might.

A Burger King wrapper sailed the length of the court on a gust. The gray sky did portend a momentous event.

Re-enacted in church with the aid of a string!

Our Lord removed His jacket and called for the ball. The Players took their positions on the Court.

The many physical advantages of the Sworn Enemies made them brazen with self-assurance,

Just as our finest actors do today when they replay the events of Our Lord's life for the delight of His followers.

for the Sworn Enemies had size, strength, and skills superior to those of Our Lord and the Two Wise Newcomers. The Sworn Enemies could out-jump the Team of Our Lord, and it was rumored that one could throw down the rock as simply as whacking a crippled mole with a generous mallet. The Sworn Enemies possessed ball-handling facility, including the cross-over dribble and the spin move. While the Sworn Enemies lacked an outside shot, they were known to be deadly in the paint, and they did mightily press their size advantage to get there. And yet the Sworn Enemies did also love themselves too much and respected Our Lord too little.

Here begins the Great Action Sequence that children re-enact on the remnants of ball courts everywhere!

Now Our Lord stood at the top of the key, dribbled two times, and passed the ball to the taller of the Two Newcomers for a give-and-go. Our Lord raised His hand for the ball as He ran to the hoop, and the Newcomer obliged with a bounce pass, which Our Lord did receive and immediately raise for a layup against the Largest Sworn Enemy.

The Largest batted the ball back into Our Lord's face and blooded His nose.

The crowd took notice without sympathy. Our

Amen!

Lord persevered.

The Largest Sworn Enemy was the most prideful of the Sworn Enemies and the instigator of the many and varied persecutions suffered by Our Lord at school and in the neighborhood. His acned face and meaty neck did haunt Our Lord's nightmares often and made Our Lord wish to vanquish him with prejudice.

Our Lord wiped His nose. He lifted himself off the ground to defend. He checked the ball at the top of the key and returned it to the Sworn Enemy, who juked left, put his elbow out, and knocked down Our Lord as he drove to the basket. The attempt by the Younger Newcomer to reach in and steal the ball was met with a shoulder to his chin, and the snap of teeth-on-teeth caused a stir in the ranks of the Manifold Witnesses as the Sworn Enemy's shot did fall through the basket.

The crowd responded with bloodthirsty shouts and raised fists.

Our Lord lifted the fallen Newcomer and encouraged him to continue the game, despite the bloody drool at the corners of his lips and the red glaze staining his teeth.

The Sworn Enemies scored thrice more with ease, two layups and a short jumper over the outstretched hand of Our Lord. Now the crowd turned against Our Lord's team for their lack of skills. When the Sworn Enemies missed shots and Our Lord's team did get the ball, the crowd jeered Our Lord for His airball from the foul line. They laughed at another shot blocked, another pass off a teammate's foot.

The wind raised its voice. The dark clouds boiled in anger. The Manifold Witnesses made movements to disperse.

And yet did Our Lord persevere. Down 6-0, *Amen!*

Perhaps this is where it occurred to Our Lord that the troubling weather recently afflicting the land could be used for Great Ends.

Our Lord received the ball after a miss. He hesitated not. His jumper from the top of the key appeared headed for a sorry miss when the First Forceful Gust did redirect it for a swish.

The Manifold Witnesses eyed the clouds yet did hesitate now to leave.

Our Lord received high-fives from the Two Wise Newcomers.

He returned to the top of the key and received a hard check to the gut from the Largest Sworn Enemy.

Amen!

Our Lord did persevere.

He repeated His quick jumper. This time the wind did propel the ball into the backboard and down through the hoop.

The Manifold Witnesses took note. They returned to their seats and perches with renewed interest. The next time, Our Lord faked the jumper and dumped off to the Larger Newcomer, who dipped under a Sworn Enemy's elbow for a layup.

The Two Magenta-Haired Girls relayed these events into their phones for the benefit of Those Who Could Not Make It.

The chill rain did fall, yet Our Lord received the weather as His due gift. He juked His Sworn Enemies into sprawling positions on the wet concrete and brought laughter to the mouths of the Manifold Witnesses. He played the wind and calculated the effects of the rain on His shots, as the storm spoke in harmony with Our Lord's passion.

This is how Our Lord did persevere.

Amen!

Yet our Lord's team did suffer more setbacks. When the Sworn Enemies were not falling to the court, they were committing flagrant fouls which they angrily denied. Their elbows flew like clubs against the chins and ribs of Our Lord and the Two Wise Newcomers, the younger of whom did also express his fear of lightning.

Technically true in the short term. It was years later that Our Lord's Great Storms washed the Earth clean.

Stand with Me, urged Our Lord, and no harm shall come to you.

The Younger Newcomer did stand, for he found strength in the words of Our Lord, even as the blood did flow from the lips and noses, as well as the knees and elbows, of Our Lord's team, staining the court red.

The Manifold Witnesses huddled together under lifted jackets and backpacks. They winced at the storm's tumult yet could not tear their eyes from the Great Upset unfolding on court.

The teams tied at 11, and then 12, and 13, with Our Lord's team playing catch-up each time. Finally, at 14, with the black sky shattering like glass and the rain tumbling like the carelessly dropped hammers of angelic ironworkers, it was decided that the next point would win the battle, and that a jump ball would determine possession.

Though the Sworn Enemies all had at least half a head on the tallest of Our Lord's team, Our Lord did not object, for He was confident now of His victory, and He had a plan. He whispered to the Two Wise Newcomers to stay back and cheat

We speak these words today to remind our believers to remain open to Our Lord's blessings.

toward the middle on defense and be prepared to receive the ball from an unexpected source.

As Our Lord and the Largest Sworn Enemy stood across from each other at the top of the key with the rain battering their cheeks and blowing into their eyes and testing the musicality of the ball with fillips to its roundness, Our Lord knew three things: first, He would lose the jump ball; second, the Largest Sworn Enemy would call for the ball after swatting it to a teammate; and third, the Largest Sworn Enemy would then drive the lane, elbowing aside Our Lord to attempt the decisive shot for his personal glory.

The Manifold Witnesses pumped their fists and shouted, now firmly on Our Lord's side, for they did respect both His determination and His great loss of blood. From among the multitude,

One never knows which of us will be called upon in the service of Fate!

a Random One was selected to toss the ball into the air. Our Lord made no effort to out-jump His rival. He backed into the lane and waited for His prophecy to unfold.

The Largest Sworn Enemy did swat the ball to his teammate.

The crowd raised its voice.

The Largest called for the ball and received it. Though one side of his face was covered in grit from a fall to the court and his lip was bloodied, the Largest started his dribble with a smirk at Our Lord.

Our Lord crouched with his arms out. A fingernail gash colored His throat, while His left ear reddened and swelled. His elbows streamed blood across His forearms, while the blood of His knees drained onto His socks, making stains for which He would later be persecuted by His worldly parents.

The storm made its voice heard, and Our Lord embraced the beauty of its awesome powers to cleanse.

The Sworn Enemy faked a move to his left. Our Lord did not bite.

The Sworn Enemy crossed over between his legs and drove to the basket.

Our Lord slid over and blocked the Enemy's path. He knew the Largest would not give up the ball.

The Sworn Enemy spun back to the middle and attempted to hook Our Lord with his thick arm and shove Him aside.

Our Lord slid into the lane and avoided the Enemy's grasp.

The Largest kept driving. He had no choice now but to plow into Our Lord, just as Our Lord had prophesized.

The Manifold Witnesses did see this and gasp. For no one had ever before taken a charge from the Largest Sworn Enemy. The Largest had size and bulk beyond all others who played the courts, with a meanness of spirit and limb that imperiled any who might test him. He had twice been held back in school. His father was rumored to whip him with *nunchakus* to toughen him.

Yet Our Lord did stand boldly in his way,

Years later, Our Lord did harness these powers to smite the world for its own good, bringing peace and goodwill to all Believers.

prepared to take the charge and give victory to His team. This is how he persevered.

Amen!

Though surprised by His actions, the Largest was determined to make Our Lord pay a heavy price. He drove a forearm up under Our Lord's chin and delivered a knee to Our Lord's thigh.

The Manifold Witnesses gasped and brought their hands to their mouths. A lightning strike went unnoticed.

Yet in the Sworn Enemy's haste to injure Our Lord he became careless with the ball, which our Lord did anticipate.

As Our Lord was shoved with great force to the rain- and blood-soaked concrete, the ball went flying down the lane and delivered itself into the hands of the Younger Newcomer, who had obeyed Our Lord's command to cheat to the middle. The Younger Newcomer received the ball and knew what to do. By the pick-up rules of this court he did not have to take the ball back and check it, as it had not touched the rim. He raised the ball over the heads of the stunned Enemies for an easy layup.

Like grace!

As we say to our children, "Go forth unchecked! For your life has not yet touched the rim!"

This is how he gave victory to Our Lord's team.

The crowd jumped to its feet and shouted. The sky flashed harmoniously. Fists were raised. The women cried with joy as they rushed onto the court to attend Our Lord, Who lay flat on His back with His bloody elbows and bloody chin and bloody scalp washing the court around Him in purifying shades.

Our Lord had taken the charge for His team and vanquished His foes. He had taken the charge for us all. Now, as the women gathered around him and the Sworn Enemies shuffled away in defeat, Our Lord's mouth opened with joy, and He did taste the sweet cool rains of His Wondrous Triumph. This is how it was.

Amen!

Weighing of the Heart

"Behold, thy lips are set in order for thee,
so that thy mouth may be opened."
—Egyptian Book of the Dead

I'm out driving one day and this girl comes floating along the side of the road—riding air, a clean three inches over the gravel. She takes little steps, though it doesn't look like she has to. Just bounces and glides, bounces and glides, like a ghost who's just become a ghost and still doesn't know it.

She isn't hitching and doesn't look my way. I brake for her anyway. This is the middle of nowhere, the eternal flatness where somebody once took a big stamper and stamped it all to dirt.

I spit my gum out, pull over into the dust, and crack the passenger door.

"Funny sort of locomotion there, if you don't mind my saying."

She wears a leather skirt down almost to the knees. Her sleeveless blouse, faded from green, shows off her tattoo: a small white feather like a stray fluff of goose down that tumbled out of the sky and settled between her shoulder freckles.

She reaches for the door handle, changes her mind, then changes it again and asks where I'm headed.

"Generally speaking," I say, "nowhere at all. But I can be persuaded to alter my route."

She grabs the frame and pulls herself in, has trouble with the heavy door. "California, please," she says, persuading me with her smile and her dusty blues, pale as air.

I look straight west, trying to picture it, but see only the dirt pressing out, mingling somewhere with the old empty vault. "Can't say I've been to California, unless it was late at night one time and I cut through a piece of it without really knowing."

She says nothing. There are more words in there but she keeps them to herself.

I ease back onto the two-laner. "Okay," I decide, "it's California. But I'd like to ask you a question first, if I may."

She's floating above the seat the way she floated down the road, her sandals hanging above the floorboard, tremoring with the big V8 and the rattle of half-crushed soda cans.

"That's personal," she says, folding her arms.

"What? I haven't asked you anything yet."

"You were gonna ask me how I came to be on the side of the road."

"Not at all. What's past is past. I was only interested in your walking style. I've never seen a floater outside a ghost movie."

Now her face winds up and she puts her hands to her eyes and sobs, sucking in her breath and catching it short. Every time her shoulders twitch, she notches up a little higher off the seat until her head bumps the nappy roofliner.

I start to wonder if I ought to set her back on the road. After all, she was floating sweet as suds without me. Except when I hear those sobs and watch the straw hair spilling over her fingers, I don't have the heart for it, though the open road and my carefree driving now look sadly endangered.

Here's how it is: I've put long miles between me and old times, but once in a while it feels like nothing at all. I'll be driving for days, paying close attention, testing myself even here in the stamped-out flats where the land's been muzzled for good. Then, late night, the old AM radio signing off and the wind pouring in like sighs, I'll lose my focus and fall into blackness, ratcheting downward till a bolt of wakefulness jacks my chin back in place. I'll steer my wheels back to the road and twist up the radio fuzz. I'll howl and twitch and claw my nails into my cheeks. I'll draw up blood with a broken toothpick. And still I tumble toward the black. Finally, I'll check my rearview, the way a guilty child checks its mother's face, knowing just what I'll find but dragged to it anyway, and what I find is my lovely wife, like all the miles I've driven have come to nothing, like the attention I've paid for years hasn't bought me a moment's peace: it's The End of Old Times, and I'm staring again at the spider web my head weaved into the windshield and apologizing to my wife, who's already joined the departed.

I've forgotten so much in the miles since the accident. I've forgotten the car I wrecked and the kind of tree I twisted it around. I've forgotten the finer points of my wife's face, and there are times I have to work hard to even call up her name. I've forgotten the town where we once made our lives, the house we kept together, the plans we made in bliss, the struggles to love and the talk between us at night. Thanks to the miles.

But I haven't forgotten my lapse of attention on our last night together and the blight of regret on its heels, and in moments of careless driving it all replays in the rearview.

And now I've invited this girl into my car when I should

have kept to the road. A natural instinct, I guess, like when someone holds out a balloon or a bouquet of flowers—you grab without thinking.

I put my hand on the girl's tattoo and try to pat out the sadness.

"I didn't mean for that to happen. I told you I wouldn't get personal, and here I must have done it anyway."

I pat until my hand gets uncomfortable there, and then I make some shushing noises while she quiets down.

"How about if I just keep my mouth shut?" I say, thinking I'll take her as far as the next highway then tell her I have a turn to hang, a new road to drive.

She nods, sucking in her lips, holding back the crying and whatever other words she's afraid of letting out. She touches her fingertips just gently to her eyes, pressing the tears before they gather momentum.

I drive. I let the road pull me along.

"See now? A lot better. We're experiencing all the pleasures the open road grants to the alert traveler."

She nods again, working her lip like gum.

A few patches of scrub slip past like refugee camps. The heat puddles and scatters on the road, fingers up in the distance. A hot breath roars in my ear. The tires and engine hum, and the dome of the world hovers high. I eye the county two-tracks, the tempting way they angle back and away from the main road, but say nothing, feeling okay now. Out driving, there are times I feel like a mummy in steel rags, but then moments like this confirm the perfection of the present tense, a flame eternal for those who attend it.

She's stopped her crying now and has one hand gripping the door handle and the other squeezing the edge of the vinyl seat, holding herself in place. Her feet still sway with every ripple in the pavement.

When she finally speaks, the words come slow, like she loves them too much and is giving them a long kiss goodbye as they pass her lips.

"One night it just happened," she tells me. "I had beautiful dreams about floating in bright blue oceans, and when I woke up I was looking down on my pillow, thick and round like I'd never slept on it. I grabbed hold of the bed and held tight, afraid I'd float out the window and up like a spirit and nobody'd ever see me again. I stayed there, floating where I was until I got up the courage to float down the hall to the breakfast table, more like paddling than walking.

"When Mamma and Daddy saw my condition they turned their heads away like I was something shameful.

"'You get yourself down on the ground this minute,' Daddy told me.

"'How'm I supposed to do that?' I asked him.

"'I ain't a voodoo doctor,' he said. 'You got yourself up there, now you get yourself back down or I'll put you out for good.'

"'Eat some crisp bacon,' Mamma said. 'That might do it.'

"But not even a whole plate of bacon helped. Soon as I let go of the breakfast table I rose up and bumped my knees and spilled the coffees, and Daddy threw down his napkin and slammed out the door.

"'Your daddy told you not to get that tattoo,' Mamma said. 'That's likely what done it.'

"I shook my head and cried, but every breath launched me higher, out of my chair then over the table. My head was knocking the ceiling when Mamma finally stopped rinsing the dishes and looked up at me. 'I always thought there was something wrong with you,' she said.

"I left home after that. Been wandering four whole days now."

I can tell the story took a toll, like she's putting the whole nasty business out on the table again, but I sort of wish she hadn't said it. It's a burden I don't need, not even my own burden, and now all I can think is, How do I shake this off?

"Well," I say. "That's some story. Yes. How do you suppose... I mean, I never heard of a live floater before. I've seen magic shows, but I don't take stock in illusion. I heard about ghosts, which I take slightly more stock in given the nature and limits of human knowledge with respect to the world's mysteries. But never a live floater. You been to a doctor? They've got all kinds of specialists these days."

She crosses her ankles, trying to keep her feet from swaying. "You know any free ones?"

"There's clinics," I say, "but none I know that tends to floaters."

We think a bit. I slap the wheel. "Ankle weights!"

"You think?"

"Sure, all we do is get something heavy around those feet and you'll be clomping around terra firma in no time."

She looks at me, fingers pressed up against the ceiling, strands of straw hair clinging to the roofliner, that little white feather tattoo bobbing with every squeak of the shocks.

"It's worth a try, anyhow. Look around my back seat, see if you can't find something heavy under those blankets or on the floor there."

She steadies herself as she spins around, then leans into the back seat and rummages through my personals, her sandals dusting my glove compartment.

"You been sleeping back here?" she asks.

"Yes," I say, knowing I'd have to speak to that at some point.

"Yes I have, but only to take naps by day. Late night's best for driving. No traffic and not much to look at, a real test of driving skills."

She totters on the seatback now, her blouse riding up her spine and her feet thumping the windshield as she reaches way down to the floor with her long skinny arms. She looks like an astronaut struggling with an outer space experiment.

"Wow," she says, "you sure do like to drive."

"Yeah, well, when I'm doing it, it's what I do, and I don't believe in doing things indifferently. Too much of that in the world these days."

She twists around, pushes herself back down in the seat, and holds out a pair of black work boots.

"Steel toes," I say. "There's the stuff. Put 'em on if you can stand the smell."

She knocks off her sandals and works her feet into the boots, heels squeaking, face scrunching, but I can tell they aren't going to work because even with one boot on and the other in her hands, her behind is still gliding across the vinyl seat.

A little curve in the road floats her over to my side.

"'Scuse me," she says, pushing against my thigh and launching herself back in place.

I clear my throat and watch a dust devil whirl across the asphalt, carrying bugs and birds and small rodents to a new life elsewhere. The sun swoops low and I flip down my visor.

The girl bangs her head on the window and dash and I cringe a little, but she finally gets the boots on. She catches her breath, staring like she's waiting for them to work their magic.

They clunk together over a bump. Then again.

She smiles with half her mouth. "They ain't ruby slippers."

Clunk.

I give her the other half of the smile. "Hmm. Don't understand it . . . those boots must weigh more than you do."

"I kind of like them," she says. "They're so big, it's almost like I'm touching the ground anyway."

I've grown to like her, and the burden doesn't seem so much. Maybe it's something to wrap me in the here and now.

The night of the accident, I had a fight with my wife, whose wondrous face I've mostly forgotten. I've forgotten the substance of the fight, too, but the fact of it remains, a tank full of fuel for miles of regret. The outcome is that my wife was giving me the silent treatment, which it seems right to believe was her habit in these situations. I didn't expect it to last so long.

We drove through the woods—maybe pine—on our way home from an evening somewhere, or else a vacation. No radio. Maybe it didn't work. Maybe we'd even fought about that.

A silent wife and a broken radio put my skills to the test, and I failed miserably. I began to nod off.

I might have thought: You'd better make nice or it's going to be a hell of a long car ride. But by then I was too tired to think. Maybe I'd even had a few drinks.

The motor hummed, the wind sighed, the tires roared softly, but the silence held its own. It wrapped me in rags, one by one, and the weight of it pressed my head gently to my chest.

If my wife had been talking to me, she might have said, Pay attention! There's a curve in the road and a tree with your name on it!

But maybe she'd nodded off, too. And so the silence drew a bead on Forever, and long miles of driving can't make me forget it.

At least now I'm awake and in the present, and the past seems a shy passenger slumped in the back seat, the riddle of this floating girl more to my liking.

"Half a solution is no solution," I tell her. "Listen, I've been down this road once or twice before and my turnaround's always been a service station up ahead. There's a man there who might set you right."

"People'll laugh when they see me float," she says.

"Not this fella. I came in once with a muffler problem and a special request. I told him I'd like to just stay in the car while he fixed it, if I might. So I drove the car onto the lift, turned up the radio, and ate my lunch ten feet in the air while he replaced the muffler. He never raised an eyebrow. And you hear that?" I ask, cupping my ear.

"Hear what?"

"See," I say. "Problem solved. A right-minded mechanic if ever there was."

She smiles. "You talk different."

I raise my eyebrows, and she repeats my last words with her shoulders thrown back and her chin tucked in, then bursts a laugh at her own impression.

"You making fun of me?" I ask, mock-serious. "I warn you, I'm a sensitive man, at the mercy of whims and fancy. I might get the urge to turn around and drop you off where I found you."

She tries to gauge me. "Sorry," she says.

"Right now I'm taken with this idea of getting you back on solid ground. Seems a worthwhile undertaking, but I need to know that you're committed to it."

"Am," she says with a nod. "When I was drifting down the side of the road, I was thinking about the things I might do in California. Be in the movies. Get my picture taken for magazines. Roller skate at the beach. Then I imagined everybody laughing at me. Even if they put me in a movie, nobody'd know it was me."

"Why's that?"

"I'd float up off the screen. At least my head would. 'Bout the only people'd know it was me'd be Mamma and Daddy, and they'd just be more ashamed than ever."

"Oh," I say, "but they can keep a close-up on your face and never bother with the floating body. Too much emphasis on a woman's body these days, anyway. Of course, there'd be problems with action scenes. Maybe then they could put ropes on you and pull you along like one of those Thanksgiving parade balloons."

"Might could," she says. "But who's going to hire an actress they've got to do all those special favors for?"

"All the stars get special favors. But you've got to show you're star material. We get you through a couple auditions and into the movies, fool 'em if we have to, then when you're a star you kick off the weights, rise up high as you like, and tell them they've got to deal with it. And they will, because then you've got star power."

She grins at that.

I pull off the road into the lone gas station that hangs out there in the flatness like a handhold for cross-country climbers. It looks to have risen from the dust, and then the dust set to work to reclaim it. What pavement there'd been has crumbled to dust. The fallen sign has been scoured to muteness by dust. Dust has driven itself into the white paint and chipped it off and peeled it back. The office window and the pump faces are clouded with dust. Dust piles up against the pumps and against the tires of the cars and the engine blocks and mufflers and the other parts that ring the station like a rusty choker.

The mechanic is sweeping the bays, slinging out dust. I pull to the pumps and give a little honk.

The man sets his broom against the wall and takes his sweet time walking over. I crank the window down all the way and put my elbow out in greeting. "Fill her up, if you would."

I watch him in my sideview. He has a good pair of sideburns—not as a fashion statement—and his gray hair follows the sunlight like a little field of sunflowers. A couple of threads hang at the pocket of his overalls where someone's name has been torn off.

"'Member me?" I call.

He clicks on the pump handle and comes forward, hand on the vinyl roof.

"'Member me? You gave me a new muffler, and I've been making good use of the peace and quiet since."

"Temporary fix," he says. "I saw lots more problems under there."

"And you told me straight," I say. "What more could a customer ask of a good mechanic?"

"Nothing," he says.

"You remember how I ate my lunch ten feet in the air, the radio playing something old and sweet?"

"Didn't notice."

"Of course, you were busy. Well, I was thinking about that today—tell you why in a moment—and I was remembering how kind you were to indulge my little peculiarity. I know a mechanic's got a proper procedure for everything—we all do—and my staying in the car had to go against proper procedure, let alone a state law or two."

"Mm-hmm," he says. The pump handle clicks.

"Well okay," I say, "we've got a situation here, the solution to which might involve some creative thinking that also goes against standard procedure. Beside me is a budding Hollywood starlet with a career-threatening flotation problem."

He leans down to get a look at the girl through the open window. She gives him a shy smile, which he acknowledges with a slight nod.

"Probably best to show you."

The girl obliges, pushing open the door, boots clomping like marionettes.

The mechanic replaces the pump handle and comes around for a look. I slide to the passenger's side to oversee.

He stares for a moment, fists on hips, judging the space between soles and dust.

"Take off your boots," he says.

She fights to keep her balance as she pulls each one off and lets it drop, raising two little clouds that march off on the breeze.

"Now walk a bit," he says, and she takes a few deliberate steps away and back like she's testing a new pair of shoes.

The man squats for a closer look, rubs his stubble to invoke the mechanical muse, then sweeps his hand between her bare feet and the ground like he's checking for strings. She wiggles her toes nervously.

"Turn around."

She twists a bit and turns without moving her feet, and when she comes to rest he gently squeezes a heel between his thumb and forefinger. One heel, then the other, up and down, testing the firmness or the sponginess or what have you.

"Boots didn't help a bit," I offer. "Steel toes, too."

"Make any difference whether she's standing or sitting?"

"No sir," she says.

"I bet she could do a handspring, a cartwheel, and a somersault, never once touch the ground," I add.

"That's true. I done a cartwheel a couple days back, just to see."

"Mmm." The mechanic stands up, puts one hand on her shoulder, and seems to gauge the pressure against his fingertips. He lowers her gently to the ground, lets her go and catches her, does it again, like dribbling a balloon.

"I figure if it was helium it would've passed through her system by now," I say.

He steadies her and lets go, gives a decisive nod, then ambles back to the garage he was sweeping, which has already sprouted a new thin layer of dust.

"Don't you worry," I tell her, my head out the window. "He knows what he's doing."

She crosses her arms and scratches one foot with the other. The shadows inch their way east, and the air loses some warmth.

"Don't you ever get out of the car?" she asks me.

"There are necessities," I say, "but generally speaking, no. At least, not while I'm out driving."

"You're an odd bird."

"Look who's talking. You're the one with the feather. Flap your wings and you might get to California for the winter migration."

She smiles, not so self-conscious anymore. "I'm not gonna forget that you helped me," she says. "When I'm in the movies and giving interviews, or roller skating at the beach and talking to my friends, I'll tell how I owe it all to you."

I laugh. "You're star material," I tell her. "You already talk the talk."

The mechanic returns with a set of keys hooked to one finger.

"What's the prognosis, doc?"

He flips the keys up into his palm. "Follow me in the car."

When he jumps into an old convertible at the side of the building, a cloud of dust rises up around him.

"Hop in," I tell the girl.

We pull onto the road behind the mechanic and head west, farther than I've been down this road. Dusk has been set in motion. The blue sky thickens and the air stills. I roll up the windows.

Pretty soon, little teeth rise up in front of the setting sun, first I've seen of the distant mountains between here and California. I'm about to point this out to the girl when she jolts me, grabbing my sleeve and shouting, "Look there! Look there!"

I take a deep swallow, my arm hairs on end from the fright she gave me.

She's pointing to an old drive-in that backs up to a curve in the road, the huge screen like a dark cut-out in the evening sky. A little ticket booth stands beside it, and a wooden wall squares off the empty viewing field. Looks like ages since the last movie, and the marquee leaves no trace of its title.

A cold wave of memory passes through me, my hands shudder, and I suddenly seem to be driving the wrong direction. I've taken this project too far, strayed from my purpose, I think, and now I'm ashamed of my inattention. The dozens of heedless miles I've just driven weigh heavy on my heart, and the world feels too small.

When the mechanic pulls off the road, I follow, but when he rolls past the old ticket booth and through to the viewing field, I jump on the brakes.

The girl looks at me as the dust rises and settles. The little ticket booth stands beside us, its angled roof half-caved. No one reaches through the broken glass to take our money.

"Can't do it," I say.

"Can't do what?"

"I haven't been in a drive-in since . . . not in years. You go on in, and I'll wait right here." I lie about waiting because I don't have the heart not to.

"We gonna watch a movie here?" She looks worried.

"He'll take care of you. Just go on."

"Is he a talent scout or something?"

I can just barely see the shape of the mechanic. He leans against his car, waiting, all the way back at the projection building.

"He's a good mechanic, and he knows to go beyond the mechanical parts if that's what's called for. Now get out," I say, a little too hard. My wet palms slip on the wheel and my throat tightens up.

She looks at me like she wants to cry again, and I think she suspects the truth.

"Go on," I say.

She sniffles, but then pushes open the door and drifts on through to the viewing field, bouncing and gliding a little slower than before.

I idle in reverse, crackling the gravel, then spin the wheel when I hit the pavement. I flip on my headlights and gas it back east, trying to swallow back the miles I let slip.

The flatness everywhere rises up and darkens the sky, and now there's just the darkness and the cones of my headlamps. I crank down my window, hoping the wind and the motor will hum away my thoughts and keep my attention on the road, where it belongs.

No dice. The silence swells like an orchestra, and the wind and the RPMs and all the miles I've put behind me can't block it out. I grip the wheel hard and press the gas till the motor wails, but old times fill my rearview anyway.

After the accident, brushing glass from my hair, apologizing to my dead wife, I tried to think. I knew there was a proper procedure for the aftermath of tragedy, but I was scared and couldn't recall it—the forgetting had begun without my even trying.

I pulled my little garden shovel from out of the trunk and started digging there in the woods under the trees I could not name. My hands shook and my sweat dropped in the dirt. Things were too quiet.

I loosened the topsoil with the point and then shoveled it out, a tiny scoop at a time, the rhythm of the action and the slush of the dirt numbing me, my breath clouding the cold night air. I must have dug for hours, though the memory of it's lost. And the hole I dug couldn't have been regulation depth, maybe not even deep enough to cover her, because when I placed her in there I know I held her hand for a moment, patting it maybe, rubbing it I'm sure, double-checking her face to see what I'd done.

Silence, and then again silence. I let go.

When I'd filled the hole, I stamped down the earth as best I could, with the shovel first, slapping the ground and working up a sweat, then with my feet and my palms, trying to make it all even, like nothing had happened there. Failing, I put my fists to my forehead and cried.

I remember all that, and now I remember something else, too. In the town we once lived in and the house we once slept in, my beautiful wife and I would lie together at night and whisper. I don't remember the town or the house or the beauty of my wife or the words she whispered, but now I remember her warm breath when it passed from her lips, each breath as good as her last, and I feel it again, the way it whirls in my ear, slow and aimless, like it might linger there forever.

I crunch on the brakes and stop there in the middle of the flatness, my head on the wheel and the tears tracking down, salting my lips. I let them fall, and let the memories play as they will. It seems like all these years they've been whirling and whirling, like a whisper's breath without the whisper. Now I hear the words, too, and I finally make sense of them.

After a while, I tell myself to breathe deep. I tell myself to open my eyes.

Dusk has turned to night, and the stars drift through the vault, quiet and distant. I crank down the window and take deep breaths of the biting air. When my hands can flex and grip the wheel again, I turn the car around and mash it back to the drive-in.

At the curve in the road, little cinders of light now burst through where the dust bored holes in the screen. When I crunch past the ticket booth and onto the viewing field, I see the cone of light hanging in the air, kindling the dust.

Rows and rows of speaker poles grid the field, all of them singing the same old tune in chorus. As I idle through the field—half cement, half weeds, all dust—the music rises and falls, rises and falls as I pass the speaker poles, some of them beheaded and hanging by wires. I can hardly catch my breath.

Finally, I spot the girl up at the glowing white screen—star material, just as I thought.

She has the opposite problem she thought she would. Instead of floating off the top of the screen, she hasn't yet floated high enough, so the bottom of the screen cuts her off at the knees.

But that doesn't seem to bother her. She moves in the light like she's part of some old dance number. She jumps and kicks and cartwheels and somersaults and never once touches the ground. The mechanic put her in the movies after all, and now I'm her audience.

As I idle slowly forward, the cone of light shining above me and the chorus of speakers on either side, I seem to raise her up little by little, a matter of perspective. She jumps and kicks and throws her head back, and she waves her arms and swivels her hips, and as she rises higher on the screen, calves and ankles coming into view, the coldness seems to pass from me and I smile.

At last her bare feet are in line with the bottom of the screen, and I put on the brakes and watch for a moment. She's back on the ground now—movie ground, anyway, and that seems good enough. I can almost feel her laughter. I put my elbow out, listening to that old melody in chorus, wishing for a box of popcorn, even.

Then maybe because she kicked a little too high, or maybe because she just got carried away, she starts drifting upward little by little. She doesn't realize it at first, but after a spin move she looks down and gets scared.

I put the car back in gear and kick up the dust, trying to get to her quick. I skid to the bottom of the screen, but I can see already that I won't be able to reach her.

"Help!" I hear her yelling over the music. She keeps floating, up toward the spirits like she first feared.

I can't let her go. I think I'll take her through those saw-tooth mountains and down into California after all. I get out of the car, stumble a bit, my legs heavy from underuse, then pull myself up onto the hood. She's just out of reach and still rising.

"I won't forget you!" she yells down, tears in her voice.

I won't give up. I crouch, take a deep breath, and jump up with all I've got. I somehow get hold of one of those thin, dusty ankles. I stand there, arm stretched high, feeling as light as I ever have, like I've just been handed a balloon or a bouquet. And this time I won't let go.

A History of War in Three Parts

Revolutions

The revolutions come once a year, usually in the spring, with angry citizens pouring into the central square of our once-beautiful capital city, raising their fists and toppling statues. The best and brightest tanks are called in to restore order. They encircle the square, turrets twisting in slow arcs like curious old people sniffing the wind. Always, there will be a photograph published of a young man performing gymnastics on the tank gun. Always someone will peer into the tank gun's snout, hoping for a glimpse of the Elite Guard reported to be inside. For a while, there are celebrations. New flags are waved. Chants roll like drums through the crowd. Pockets of intensity flare where the foreign media set up cameras. Stages are built. Bands play. While speakers line up for a turn at the mic, babies are born and opposition leaders return from exile. New dances take shape over the footprints of past revolutions. Before long, there is a struggle between those who favor velvet gloves and those who favor rolling heads. Harmony turns to mistrust and mistrust to violence. A scuffle erupts and a shot that might have been a firecracker. The revolution scuttles toward its end with the help of the Elite Guard.

Of the Elite Guard, some say they are no longer human in the usual sense and are coated with metal, the same layers of bulletproof armor that protect the tanks. Some say the Guard have no faces, that they do not think or feel and have been reprogrammed by computers or torture to act mechanically in the interests of the government or as instruments of their tanks. Some say the Guard are young boys who have not yet learned to feel, or have too soon forgotten. Some say the Guard is a myth and that the tanks have no one inside. The debate is resolved only by agreement that the insides of tanks are a useless topic of discussion. The tanks are black boxes of artificial intelligence, we say, and their inner workings impossible to understand, however many young men peer down one's snout or skitter under another's smooth, hard underbelly.

Yet, from a distance, you can predict the tanks' behavior with a degree of accuracy. You can feel the moment coming, not long after the fireworks, or the gunshots, or the expanding scuffles. You can stand on a hill outside the city or look through the window of a tall hotel not far from the square and feel the moment's approach in your chest. Time ticks hard through your veins. The air dries in your throat. Individual sounds clamor into one sound, and the one sound is like a call to the tanks. Who can say whether or not the tanks receive orders from the government or take cues from the protestors? Only the tanks' behavior is certain; its incitements are beyond us.

From up close, the tanks don't act as a single force. One will jerk forward, crushing a woman slipping flowers into its treads. Another will fire .50 caliber rounds through the body of the swinging gymnast. Others will hold their positions, in the short view giving protestors the impression there's still hope. In the long view, the tanks' procession is inevitable. It's how our revolutions work: first, a few tanks inflict spotty damage; next, a promenade crushes bodies in the square. As other tanks join in, the .50 calibers flicker like precise fireworks in the night. The tanks' motors are the steady growls of lions loping after easy prey. Before long, the makeshift structures of the revolution are splintered like toys. The tanks plow rivers of silence through the screams. Bodies split open and reveal their fragile inner workings, confessing their weaknesses under the treads. Some protestors risk their own lives to carry off the injured and the dead. Others, recently mugging for the cameras, hide their faces and run. Sometimes, an international reporter will be injured or killed, damaging foreign relations in the short-term.

The square is cleared before sunrise. For a time, the tanks idle in a group, surrounded by bodies and blood. A few things will remain standing that no one could have expected. A food stall with hanging meats. A microphone stand. A portable toilet.

Bulldozers come and push the revolution's remains into a pile. The pile is burned. The tanks turn and depart.

Smoke tendrils up from the empty square, and those in sniffing distance must close their windows against the smell.

Who will be first to walk through the new square? Someone must. In this case, a man with an old gray hat and ill-fitting clothes. He takes a few steps with his hands in his pockets. Looks around. Takes more steps. Scratches himself. He seems to be chewing something. Who can tell what's driving him? He cuts through one corner of the square and eventually zig-zags to the center. At one time, there was a fountain at the center where birds and people congregated, throwing things in and taking things out. Some of that fountain's tiles still remain, their hand-painted images of doves and flowers now dirty with footprints, black stains, tracks. Still, it's evident that people danced here. They had a revolution. They let themselves think they could predict the inner workings of tanks. For a time, everything felt new. They forgave themselves and each other for old misdeeds. They soaked the land in crazy optimism.

The man stands on their footprints and wonders how they could have let themselves think this. He wonders what they had inside them that could prompt them to stare down the black tunnel of a tank barrel, knowing it will explode in their faces.

He places a shoe on one of their tracks, his other shoe on another, and makes his way across the rest of the square in a kind of dance. A step forward and two to the side. But there is no music, and the choreography reveals much less than he'd hoped.

The General

Famously, they fell upon their swords when they could not defeat the invading army, leaving the occupying force unchallenged and the citizens to be brutalized, to be raped and tortured and maimed and drawn and quartered, or tarred and feathered, or whatever form of humiliating and excruciating torture was available and popular at that time.

All fell, that is, except the general, who did not need the ritual suicide to secure his place in history. The general only pretended, allowing the sword to slip between his arm and torso like an actor in a community theater who might be forgiven for not really wanting to kill himself for the sake of verisimilitude. *I am only a general,* he thought, as the sword sliced through the sleeve of his uniform, *which is to say that I am only generally engaged in things, only generally to blame for the deaths and the general defeat of the general forces of the alliance. It does not mean that I, for example, am specifically to blame for any of the individual deaths* (so many of which he had witnessed the horrific specifics—the last breaths gasped through red, red roses that bloomed on slit throats and gaping chests; the last words still hanging in the air and then falling suddenly under the unexpected weight of becoming Last Words but creating anyway just the kind of showstopper performance that a general, for example, would have desired in victory but now must settle for in defeat, with the bloodied multitudes falling in military precision upon the swords they had carried halfway across a continent through trenches and razor wire as dead weight, not useful in battle and not designed for anything but the falling on of which they were now specifically engaged in). *Nor,* he thought, *does it mean that I am to blame for the specific grieving of the individual families,* many of whose tears would anyway be washed away in blood, silenced by rape, evaporated by torture. *Nor am I responsible for my own specific act of cowardice,* the completion of which is fast approaching. *I am only assuring a general conclusion,* he thought, *to a battle already lost in specifics not specifically of my own doing.*

And in such manner the general struck the soil, his head bouncing in the general fashion of his dramatically obedient and now suddenly discharged troops (though his bounce was a bit livelier perhaps, the grunt and the curse not cursed to be his Last Words, thank God), whereafter he waited a few moments with his eyes closed until all the last words were exhaled and then fell in the dirt or were swept away by the wind, and a general and strangely affecting silence settled on the open plains.

Unnoticed, he dusted himself off and left the battlefield, conceding the shame it would be if there were no one left to write a general history of this war and place it squarely in the general scheme of things.

The Posse

The first sign is a cold damp sizzle on the skin. Then a low-frequency pulse in the ears, a pressure on the skull. The mouth goes dry. A flickering 30-watt glow and, seemingly all at once, raised voices everywhere, utterances unfamiliar except as the language of rage. Their crude weapons flash into view. Planks and tree limbs with bent nails. Rusty chains, whipped and swung. Bayonets on useless rifles. Broken glass. Homemade explosives. Hopelessness. Entire cities are overwhelmed before the threat even registers. Others see news reports and try to mount a defense. They gather under billboards at the city limits. They block off highways and fan out into the woods, their weapons more sophisticated. Laser-guided automatic rifles. Grenade launchers. Heat-seeking vitriol. The conviction of inherited wisdom. They keep watch in towers. They patrol in armored trucks. In their confusion, they're quick to shoot and sometimes kill their own. When the glow approaches, they mistake it for a three-quarters moon and realize too late for tactical maneuvers. They fire into it, though there is nothing to hit but flames. The noise is a piercing murmur, a collapsing wall of nails, a dozer blade.

When a swath is cut through the countryside, the smaller towns rise up out of years of neglect and join hands in nervous indignation. *Not here, not now. Not us.* They fashion their own crude weapons. Edger blades and skewers, pole saws, weeders, staple guns and bolt cutters, pruning shears, butcher knives, items passed along the circuit of yard sales and flea markets now elevated to engines of war. They sandbag their homes and watch the scenes on the news, the smoldering path of destruction taking aim. *Not here, not now*, they say, sharpening blades, cleaning a family shotgun. *Not us.*

And then comes the cold electrical charge and the distant voices. The shouts and metallic scrapes. Pulses of noise like labored breaths. They part their curtains to the dusty glow, the flashes of raised fists and clubs that vanish before they come into focus. A chaos of rage. When trees fall and buildings fall they know in an instant their sandbags will not hold up, so they go out to meet the enemy with their yard-sale weapons, marching through the streets, their indignation blooming into blind hatred. *Not here, not now. Not us.* The voices shoot from all directions, and flames light the horizon. Are they inside it, already at war? Unsure where to aim or what to yell, they swing their tools and scream, their voices indistinguishable from the raging, injured screech of the enemy. They kill each other. They kill themselves. They split open skulls with the same tools they used to trim their lawns. They slice through arteries with the same blades that once trimmed their beards. They prune off arms and legs and gouge out eyes. They maim and murder. They blast into crowds. The blood on the streets and on their clothes is a sign of progress. When their weapons snap or splinter or jam, they tear off their shirts and strangle. They flay with leather belts. Crush skulls with steel-toed boots. Tear off hunks of flesh with their bare hands. They are moving forward. Something is being done. The noise does not confuse them anymore because they've become an essential part of it. They are meeting the enemy head-on. And when their tools are gone and their arms exhausted, they bring out ever stronger weapons. Their religion. Their pride. Their love of country. Their community bond. Their primal desire to murder the unknown. These weapons empower them against their own self-doubts, so that more blood is spilled and even with dwindling numbers they seem to be winning. In their final surge to victory, they go door to door and demolish their own houses and stores. They dig up the graves of their ancestors and scatter the bones. Dying themselves, they pull their children out of their beds and send them out into the bloody, quieting streets as reinforcements.

The children rub their eyes and stare at the town that has been ruined to protect them, the house demolished to keep them safe, the bed torn apart to give them a place to sleep, the parents who have killed each other to keep the family whole. They feel a cold dampness on their skin, and they rub their own arms to keep warm. *Here,* they say. *Now. Us.*

Chomolungma

Base Camp. Mother and Jennifer collapse on the slope as Father stands on a rock and gazes back down the trail. Two of the hired Sherpas are already unpacking and setting up tents. The mountains are a huddled mass of white-robed gods, the upper-level winds blowing auras off their pointed skulls. The cold thin air dissolves like a wafer on the tongue. It's like nothing back home, a lofty spirit-walk their bodies are privileged to have joined, if only for a few weeks.

Minutes pass. At last Father spots William, droop-shouldered, eyes to the rocks, trailing the third Sherpa and a yak. He slowly claps his hands. "His Highness at last!"

William says nothing.

"It's one thing to be late for school or soccer practice, but do you have any idea what happens if you fall behind on Everest? Monsoon season is coming!"

"I don't care," William murmurs.

"I didn't hear you."

"Nothing."

"What happens is, you can forget the summit. You can forget soccer practice, too. And all those precious afternoons alone in your room with stolen liquor and dirty magazines and World of Nerdcraft. Up here, timing's a matter of life and death. Do you know what a whiteout's like on the Lhotse Face at 24,000 feet? Do you have any idea what hurricane-force winds can do to an exposed climber? Do you?"

"I don't care either," says Jennifer. "I hate this. I'm eighteen and I'm not even legally obligated to spend time with you people. *And* I'm missing the Alterna-Prom. I finally had an outside chance at High Priestess!"

"Quit whining," Father says. "All of you! Does anyone even understand what this is about? After your mother here put her hand down the pants of the office temp and squeezed his Johnson in plain view of pretty much anyone driving slowly past the office window and not even spying but casually glancing inside, the fate of the family fell to me. *Me.* I could have just let us all fall apart. I did not. I regrouped. I planned. I understood the need for desperate measures. I went for broke."

"Did you ask *me*?" Jennifer says. "You never ask *me*. Nobody does."

"We didn't ask you if you wanted to be born, either. But here you are. Deal with the consequences."

"Everyone else does," says William.

"Shut up, pimple-butt."

"Haven't we come far enough?" Mother asks. "My legs are so tired. I think my organs are failing. My ears are like a Play-Doh factory for my swelling brain."

"Buck up. You of all people. William, did you load up my Lucky Katana ice axes with the solar-heated grips? The ones those equipment brokers sold me in Gorak Shep?"

William shrugs. "I don't know. We have the other ones."

"I don't want the other ones. Now go back and get them."

"What? That's like three hours each way!"

"We'll wait."

"Seriously?"

"Seriously."

William kicks the ice and hurts his foot. "Can't I do anything right?"

"You tell me."

"Does he really have to go?" Mother says. "This whole thing is ridiculous."

"He's got to learn."

"Then let's go with him. And not come back."

"Not a chance. Hustle up, Will! Back by nightfall!"

William slumps back down the trail like he's dragging a rock. The others watch. Father shakes his head.

"You know the Sherpas are laughing at us," Mother says. "They're pointing and laughing. They're enjoying themselves at our expense. We paid two hundred thousand dollars and came all the way to Nepal just to give them a show."

"Nonsense," Father says. "They're laughing at Jennifer's vampire make-up. Couldn't you leave that junk behind?"

"God! I can't even breathe up here and you're telling me you hate my make-up! Don't even talk to me ever again!"

"Fine, I'm the hater. I hate everything. That's why I'm spending my retirement money on family time."

"Oh Christ," says Mother. "Always the martyr."

The Khumbu Icefall. A slow-motion flood sweeps house-sized ice sculptures downstream in the glacier. The enormous blocks and pinnacles crack and split without warning. New crevasses open between them. Older crevasses, hidden by thin bridges of snow, make deep, narrow *punji* pits for unwary climbers. Aluminum ladders are bound together and placed over the crevasses. Guide ropes are stretched. Climbers step carefully across the ladder-bridges, their attention on foot placement rather than the chasms between rungs. The wind blows. The ladders bounce and sway. The ice towers crackle like someone's twisting them.

"Are we there yet?" says Jennifer. "Are we even close?"

"This is more about the journey," Father says.

"Can't we just get this done and go home?" says Mother.

"You agreed to this. The least you can do is have a good attitude about it."

"You gave me an ultimatum," says Mother. "I'm having serious regrets."

"Be quiet," Father says. "It's Family Time. Remember when we all joined together and made the biggest Alan Greenspan sand sculpture Nag's Head Beach has ever seen? Or when we sang 'I've Got Snow, Snow, Snow, Snow, Down in My Boots' all the way down the Highline run at Vail, even though your mother wiped out twenty-six times and the ski patrol had to tow her the rest of the way in a sled? Remember at Bryce when we all split up without rations and the game was to find our way back together before sunset?"

"Big fun," Jennifer says.

"Frankly, no," says Mother, "I don't remember a thing. But that only means the pills are working."

"Okay, I want everyone to say what they think is special about our family," says Father.

"Can I start?" says Jennifer. "This family's a joke. An actual joke. Except there's no punch line, so it's like the set-up for a joke someone else has to finish. After we're all dead. Which is soon."

"Can we at least wait till William gets across the ladder?" Mother asks.

"Hustle up, Will!" Father calls. "We're having a family powwow over here!"

William's knees are shaking. His crampons scuttle the sides of the ladder like nervous crabs. He can't help but imagine a fall into the deep, narrow blackness—how he could lose his balance from wind or nerves or icy metal and tumble into the wedge, where he'll be popped and crushed like an egg between tectonic plates, sort of a cosmically apt illustration of the way he's been ground between angry parents his whole life, but terrifying nonetheless. He grips the guide ropes tight with his thick black gloves. When the ladder trembles in the wind he freezes, and for a moment it looks as if he's going to go over like a toppled statue. He finds his balance, takes another step, another. William's always been the cautious one; he didn't take the training wheels off till he was ten. But is he really so cautious, or is everyone else just a reckless idiot?

Father claps his hands. "Another grand entrance from Will the Great!"

"I nearly died," William says.

"Life is full of challenges. Buck up."

"Or *off*," mumbles William.

"I didn't hear you."

"Nothing."

"Listen, I told the Sherpas to go on ahead and fix the ropes and ladders for us. That will give us some time to ourselves. Why don't you start?" he says to Mother. "It's only appropriate."

"Let's get something straight," Mother says. "My guilt has limits. My guilt does not reach the Everest summit. My guilt goes up approximately 19,000 feet, which if I'm not mistaken is right about here…"

Mother takes one step up the snow bank in the shadow of a leaning pinnacle and stabs the ice with her crampon points to steady herself.

"What new stunt is this?" Father asks.

"Guilt requires oxygen, and there's not enough at this level to support it. Look."

She takes a step down.

"Here, guilt."

She takes a step up.

"Here, no guilt. I've entered the guilt-free zone. It's that simple."

The icefall makes a muffled noise like there's someone chipping away from the inside.

"Mom, quit making a fool of yourself," Jennifer says.

"That comment would have an effect under 19,000 feet," says Mother.

"Kids, remember how we learned that oxygen deprivation causes dangerous delusions? That's what your mother's experiencing now. Pay no attention to her crazy talk."

"I've never felt more clear-headed," Mother says.

"See, kids?" says Father.

"Can we keep moving?" Jennifer asks. "I mean, has anyone even noticed how extremely ridiculously cold it is and how the air is like negative air that actually vacuums the oxygen out of your blood and how we're all going to die anyway because our Sherpas are about thirteen and can't even tie their shoelaces?"

"I'm finally seeing everything as it really is," says Mother. "It's only the latest in a long line of guilt trips that began when I married you in the first place."

"Mother's talking too much and wasting her oxygen," says Father.

"It's true," says Mother. "You kids might as well hear the truth."

"Lalalalalala! Stupid family revelations! I'm not listening!" Jennifer says. She puts her North Face gloves to the side of her head. She decorated them with glittery silver skulls.

"I felt guilty that I'd rejected your father five times already," Mother says. "So I finally gave in and married him. He knew I'd give in because I was pliable back then. I knew he knew, and I took the easy route anyway. It's all clear to me now."

"Lalalalalala," Jennifer says. "Tell your family secrets to someone who cares!"

"Great," says Father. "Well now that that's all cleared up, how about you, William?"

"I kissed that office temp out of guilt, too," Mother continues. "He reminded me of Brian, the boy I was going to marry if he'd only had the nerve to ask me all those years ago. I should have married him and didn't. The office temp was sweet and shy like Brian. It didn't matter that they looked nothing alike. Brian had those thick lips and the constant pout. He had the turned-up eyebrows and the small ears. The soft hands too big for his wrists. The office temp, I don't even remember his name but I could tell he liked me, and so I kissed him because I felt guilty that he was too shy to ask. Shyness has a smell I've come to love. I wasn't really kissing him anyway. I was kissing Brian, a whole army of Brians—the ones who bag my groceries in the supermarket or hit balls against the practice wall at the tennis club, the ones all over town that throw quick shy glances at me before they climb onto their bikes and motorcycles and ride away, all those Brians who always just barely lack the nerve to tell me they love me. They've always needed a little help, and for once I gave it to them."

There's a pause. Jennifer lifts her gloves away from her ears. "Done yet?"

"Well," says Father, "squeeze a boy's Johnson and he'll tell you anything you want to hear. Awfully generous of you."

"Shit!" says Jennifer.

"One thing led to another," Mother says. "I don't feel guilty about it."

"Your mother's intent on ruining this vacation," says Father. "Just like all the others."

"I don't remember the others," says Mother.

William's not listening, his mind still deep in the crevasse. Falling, falling, then stuck. He feels now the glacial movements, the ice walls pressing against him, rolling him and squeezing him like a hand-rolled joint. And there's no way out. He'll die like this, fully conscious, his ribs snapping one by one, organs collapsing in on one another. Heart constricted until it flutters like a crushed moth. And then he remembers the special tools he went all the way back to the tea house in Gorak Shep to retrieve. The solar-heated grips would warm his hands. It's not too late! There's still room to grab them from Father and angle a swing at his head! Still time to free himself of the slow torture!

Someone else's head appears from behind an ice block. Then three more. Another expedition team, heading back down the mountain. They use the fixed ropes to descend the ice.

"Excuse me!" says the first, a tall man with a thick dark beard. "You all are making an awful lot of noise. You're endangering the other climbers in the icefall."

"We're just pausing a moment to reflect on our family," Father says.

"Well could you do it somewhere else?"

"Ah, I see. Didn't make the summit, I guess," Father says.

"That's none of your bloody fucking business."

"Take me with you!" Jennifer yells. "Please! They've kidnapped me! They're trying to kill me!" She pulls on the man's parka sleeve.

The man shakes her off. "For God's sake, your lips have turned black," he says. "Get some help. All of you."

Two more men appear at the top of the ice block, carrying a stretcher between them. Two others climb halfway up to help. There's a careful handoff and some whispered words. The man on the stretcher groans softly.

"He's looking worse," says the first man. "We'd better hurry."

As they pass, the man on the stretcher writhes in slow motion. His face is puffy and dark. His swollen lips are split, his eyes bandaged.

A moment of quiet as the other expedition negotiates their first steps on the ladder bridge. Even the icefall shows respect.

"At least we've got our health," William says.

"Suck-up," says Jennifer.

William lifts his trembling arm and meets his dad's glove for a high five. He's certain he's going to free himself. He sees a glimmer of light now, a way out.

"Anyone see how our Sherpas up there stopped on the ledge to watch?" Mother asks. "They're thinking they should be paying *us* for this trip. They're wishing they had us on film to show their whole village."

"Let them laugh all they want. Who's going to laugh when we reach the summit and plant the family flag?"

"Family WTF?" asks Jennifer.

"It's tucked into my pants for safekeeping," Father says. "I was going to make it a surprise at the summit, but it looks like you and your mother need the extra motivation."

Mother feels a pang like a tiny crash in an empty warehouse.

It's encouraging that she still had anything left to break.

"I think we've rested long enough," Father says. "What say we get a move on?"

"Hey, Dad," William says. "Want me to carry your ice axes for you?"

Nightfall. Jennifer lies awake staring at the red nylon ceiling, its color fading in the deepening twilight. There's no wind, and she can hear the voices of other expedition teams. Mother, Father, and William are asleep. Eyes shut, breathing deep like there's nothing wrong with this stupid world or their stupid places in it. Jennifer knows better. It's stupid. The trip's stupid, the mountain's stupid, pretty much everything to do with climbing is stupid. Why risk your life to be cold and out of breath? To stand at the top of a stupid mountain just so you can tell everyone you did? Like everyone's going to be *so* impressed. *Hey, we took a family vacation just so our father could try to kill us without going to jail for it!* Awesome! As soon as she graduates, she's moving out.

But why wait?

She gets to her knees, crawls over William's chubby legs tucked in the sleeping bag, and unfastens the Velcro flap. Goodbye, family. Their bags are zipped to the chin. They look like mummies. The tent's just an old chamber full of mummies or soon-to-be-mummies, and she's going to avoid their curse.

The Sherpas are out in the cold. They've got their arms together, singing and kicking their legs like drunk chorus girls. They chant a few words until one of them starts giggling. It takes them a minute to notice Jennifer. The shorter guy stumbles over as he pulls something out of his waistband.

Jennifer takes a step back.

He holds out a stainless steel flask that catches the twilight and glows. He's all smiles. Jennifer can't decide if the guy is thirteen or thirty-five. His glistening teeth lean against each other for support.

She takes the flask. If she survives, the smell of alcohol will always bring her comfort and warmth. She already knows it.

The Valley of Silence. Two of the Sherpas lead the team through the Western Cwm. The comparatively gentle incline provides little relief, as the windless valley forms a heat trap that saps a climber's energy. The cwm's central glacier is mauled by deep lateral crevasses, forcing the expedition to sidle along the base of Nuptse, where rockfalls and avalanches are a constant threat.

"It's almost too easy," says Father. "I'm barely winded and feel strong as an ox. Where's the struggle? We could use more struggle. The struggle's what brings us together."

"In that case we could have quit our jobs and slowly starved to death in the comfort of our own home," says Mother.

"I've already quit mine," Father says. "Or I've been fired, depending on how you look at it."

Mother is too tired to ask.

Jennifer has fallen behind. Gloves off, she's holding hands with the third Sherpa, the shorter one. He's either growing a moustache or has already failed at it. His lower lip is thick with Jennifer's black lipstick, and someone's drawn black ankhs under his eyes. Like tears of life, Jennifer told him last night.

"Look who's dragging this time," Father calls. "Hustle it up, Jen! There's a rival expedition catching up to us."

"Since when is it a race?" Mother asks.

"It's not. But it looks bad if we can't hold our position."

"I can't possibly move any faster," Mother says. "My leg meat's gone rancid and my skin has no feeling. I don't even remember why we're here."

"Think 'Johnson,'" says Father.

Jennifer keeps her eyes on the mountaintops on either side of the high valley, then turns to her new boyfriend and whispers something in his ear. They share a laugh. His mouth is a starry-night negative, constellations of mysterious black flecks against a yellow backdrop. The two of them stumble in the snow, catch their balance, laugh again.

Father stops, hands on hips, to give her a disapproving look that she can't see through his tinted goggles. "Just what do you think you're doing?" he asks.

Jennifer stumbles past. "Excuse me, who are you people?"

The Sherpa laughs. He's a few inches shorter than Jennifer and wide around the middle.

"She's doing this to spite us," Father says.

"You catch on quick," says Mother.

William watches the rocks rain off the Nuptse face, small black polka dots blossoming against the pale sky and the snowcapped peaks. They are little pieces of fate that fall all over the world in the form of car wrecks, stray bullets, deadly airborne germs, or twisters doodling over the plains and flicking aside houses like stray ants. They're trajectories of death. Up here it's just amazing how clearly you can see the black dots falling, as if the air has thinned to a loose mesh, and with every step up the mountain, the gaps widen and the secret nature of the world reveals itself more clearly in the form of those falling shapes. They're little black holes that swallow up lives. One falls three feet to the right of Father. A bigger one five yards in front. Father's oblivious. He could have his head crushed at any moment, and he acts like he's got a shield, like he's going to live forever.

A melon-sized black rock falls into the snow and ice not four feet in front of Father and splits in two as his head might have done. What is wrong with this world that so many rocks can miss such a big target?

"Shouldn't we get moving?" William says.

"That's the spirit," says Father.

William feels the weight of his new wisdom, the burden of too much insight. Plus, he's got one of Father's ice axes hooked around his elbow. That's a burden, too. The burden of awesome possibility. And the clothes beneath his parka—starting with his two-sizes-too-big Fruit-of-the-Loom briefs and his one-size-too-small GWAR t-shirt—are drenched in sweat. They tug at his skin with each step. Tonight they'll freeze solid. With every step, he accepts these burdens anew. A continual affirmation of purpose. He can see now how life is sharpened to a dagger on these high peaks. One either uses it to pierce the stupid façade, or else one gets clumsy and falls on it. So it goes.

"Where's your Sherpa," Father asks later when he catches up to Jennifer.

"God, he's not *my* Sherpa. That's so racist! The Sherpas don't *belong* to anybody, especially not us."

"We're paying them."

"Nobody should have to take people like us up the sacred *Chomolungma*. We're defiling the holy goddess mother of the world and oppressing their culture just being here! We're like a walking plague! We suck!"

"He's already given you the usual boyfriend brainwash," Father says. "So why aren't you with him now?"

"I'm giving Tashi his space. I'm not going to invade his life like we're invading their country."

"You didn't even crack the guide books I gave you."

"In Sherpa society, women can have as many husbands as they want."

"Here we go."

"Sherpas barter and share, and no one ever goes hungry. They all care for each other. It's like a big commune, except it's not communist. It's like a Craigslist forum in real life. And the only thing women have to do is give the men a little space to play cards now and then."

"Sounds swell."

Evening. Sunset crawls up the mountainsides until the cone of Everest stands out like an orange candy corn. Expedition teams huddle around their bright panels of stretched nylon. They light cooking fires and check tomorrow's weather reports. They chatter on satellite phones in eleven languages and blog on their laptops. They share stories and negotiate rope-setting fees with other teams. They warm themselves on expectation.

Inside the family tent, Mother and Father are already asleep, sucking in deep quick breaths that rattle like pachinko balls before falling down their throats. William lies perfectly still, staring at the glowing red nylon with a slight grin as if reaching one satisfying conclusion after another.

"Brian, is that you?" Mother murmurs in her sleep. She's dreaming she's in a large empty vault, possibly a warehouse, though she can't see the walls, and the high ceiling with its dim fluorescent lights is obscured by a lowering haze. Is it a cloud of poison gas? She's alone in there, and yet outside the walls (wherever they are) lives a team of Brians, actually a whole society of Brians, whose quiet desire for her is their whole reason for existence, the exclusive subject of their thoughts, even their currency of exchange. They relate their thoughts and fantasies of her in return for sustenance, and they sustain themselves only to think of her. It's like a commune of unsatisfied desire. How can she tell them she's not worth it? How can she say that even though someone else led her into the vault, she's the one who locked the door? It's not true that she's lost her guilt, at least when it comes to the City of Brians. The world's become irreconcilable. How can it go on this way?

"Johnson," murmurs Father. "Johnson."

There's a late expedition emerging now from the Western Cwm, a single-file line of dark figures climbing from the black valley up to the gray plateau. They go unnoticed as they slip into camp. In the fading light, their faces are pale gray, their eyes dark and deep-set. One turns her head to the summit, and something on her lower lip catches the light.

"Trip?" she calls. It's a young voice. "Trip Six?! Trippy!"

Jennifer squeezes through the flap of the family tent. "Shadowgirl? Are you serious! Oh my God!"

High-pitched screams stir up snow on the high peaks. Lhotse responds with a small avalanche and rockfall, just noise and shadows in the dim twilight.

"Talon! Raven! Lilith! Vlad! Oh my God, I love you guys," Jennifer says.

There's a group hug in the snow.

"Trip, we knew you were going to miss Alterna-Prom, so we brought it to you."

Raven holds out an earbud so they can share her music as they dance in the snow.

"You guys are the best!" says Jennifer. "I want you to meet

someone. Hey, Tashi!"

Soon they're drinking and dancing with the Sherpas and sharing gossip from school. Later, they all take hits of oxygen like it's nitrous oxide.

The Lhotse Face. The slope is like a mounded plain of blue ice and snowdrifts pitched steep. Climbers must kick their points into the glacial ice, pull themselves up on the fixed ropes, and steady themselves with another kick. At 24,000 feet, a climber might not be thinking clearly. His sense of balance may falter. He may lean back too far and slide. He may have thought he'd clipped his carabiner to the rope at the last anchor. He may have thought the rope was secure, or may not have noticed how frayed it was. He may not even notice he's falling at first. He's suddenly disoriented, looking up at the sky, and he's not sure if he's moving or stationary. He experiences a pleasant floating sensation until he feels a jagged rock tear across his back and starts tumbling. It's over just like that.

The team stands at the base and looks up. The wind has kicked up and the sky is white-gray with swirling snow that whips off the ice.

"You said the Sherpas were already here," Mother says.

"No, I said they'd already left," Father says. "I didn't say where."

"Who *are* the Sherpas anyway?" Mother says. "Were we supposed to have them over for dinner?"

"I hate the Sherpas," says Jennifer.

"Oh. In that case I'll just rescind the invitation."

"End of romance?" Father asks.

"Men are the same everywhere," Jennifer says. "Even the Sherpas."

"These guys aren't even Sherpas," Father says. "I got a discount. I think they're from Pakistan."

"Great," says Jennifer. "You got the *discount* Sherpas!"

"Hey, times are tough. Our stocks took a hit."

"I don't even know who you're talking about," Mother says.

"Did you know that Sherpas make their wives sleep outside with the yaks?" says Jennifer.

"Say no more," Father says. "I can put two and two together."

"Did you know that Sherpa men seem to prefer dumb ugly bitches to intelligent and attractive women?"

"We'd better start climbing. Sun's almost up."

"It's a total fact that Sherpa men are so naïve they can't even see when they're being used."

"More avalanches when the sun warms the ice," says Father.

"And they act like they like bitchy women, like they've got mother issues or something."

"He's not even a Sherpa," Father reminds her. "Will, where's my other axe?"

A bank of gray clouds darkens the morning sky and blocks the sunrise. A light snow falls.

"The Sherpas took it," William says. He wonders if he can get ahead of Father high on the Lhotse face and cut the rope with something. He wonders if there's freedom at the top of the world.

"They really are awful people," says Father.

"But they're not even Sherpas," says Jennifer.

"Either way, we're not having them to dinner," says Mother.

The Lhotse Face, Part II. The wind blows. The snow falls heavy. Father checks everyone's carabiners at the anchor points. A couple of teams have turned back and encouraged the family to do so too: The weather reports are bad. Monsoons are coming early, bringing blizzards and high winds. You don't want to be stuck on Everest with no visibility.

"We enjoy a challenge," Father tells them.

"I hope you enjoy killing yourself, too, fucking idiot," says the leader of the second expedition.

"We don't even have any oxygen!" laughs Father.

When the rival team has descended out of hearing range, Mother taps Father's crampon with her ice pick.

"Isn't oxygen the stuff you're supposed to breathe?" Mother asks.

"We had a few bottles. They're missing."

"I hate that you're always forgetting things," Mother says.

"I think the Sherpas took them. Don't fall behind, Will!" Father calls down the steep slope.

Will is thinking along the lines of the leader of the second expedition, hoping that Father enjoys killing himself. The convergence of sentiment makes him wonder if people can read his thoughts up here. Seems like his skull has become more permeable to take in the air it doesn't get from his lungs. He's widening his intake, expanding his head, until anyone within fifty feet of him is part of his brain and thus included in his thoughts. Does that include family? Was that the kind of togetherness Father was talking about when he popped the lock on William's room, clapped his hands together and said, "Guess what, son? We're taking a family trip to Everest!"

"I want to kill you," Mother tells Father.

(Yes, it does; it does include family.)

"Why this time?"

"You locked us in this cold room, and you didn't even tell me to bring my sweater."

"You don't need a sweater, dear. You have thermal underwear. A down suit. Gore-tex. I'm surprised you're not hot."

"My skin is plasticized. Someone's got the ceiling fan on. Turn it off, please. Look at all these stupid Lawrence Welk bubbles like we're inside Grandma's TV. So fake. I can barely hear Brian knocking."

"Get a grip. We've still got thousands of feet to go."

"I'll get that," Mother says. "I don't want to be late to the prom. If you'll just please for God's sake unlock the door!"

Mother lets go of the rope and reaches behind her into the gray air.

"What the hell are you *doing*?"

She takes a step in the direction of nothingness and slides down the rope into Jennifer, who slides into William, who is pushed against a rock. It's chaotic and slow. The ice chunks from their fall tumble down the face of the mountain into the gray-white air below. Jennifer totters backwards and flails her arms. Only the rope catches her. Father can feel its tug and holds tight to his ice axe, straining.

"I'm coming right down!" Father calls.

He backs slowly down the steep slope. The clouds thicken. There's no bottom or top to the mountain now. They're in the steep endless middle of the tallest part of the world. There's enough wind to swirl the snow, more creepy than dangerous. And the sound carries well. They can hear each other's breaths.

"Everyone okay?"

"My mind is blubbery!" Mother shouts.

"I want to go home!" yells Jennifer.

"My corsage—she's crushed!" adds Mother.

William keeps his focus. It's important to be alert. Aware. Alive to the limited possibilities the world offers.

"That was exciting, at least," says Father. He swings his one Lucky Katana ice axe and jabs his crampons into the ice. "Give me your hand," he says to Mother.

"No fucking way, loser. I've got plans."

"I know you do. We're making the summit."

"Not with you, I'm not. I like shy boys. Only shy ones."

"Mom, please get the hell off me!" whines Jennifer. "You're breaking my ankle! I want to go home!"

"Tough it out," says Father.

"I've been toughing it out for eighteen years!" says Jennifer.

(They're me, thinks William. They're all a part of my brain. It's going to complicate things.)

The Death Zone. "This is the Geneva Spur," Father tells them when they climb the anvil rock.

"This is the Yellow Band," he says later.

Still later: "At last we're on the South Col."

"No one cares," Jennifer says. "No one cares as of a long time ago."

"At least you've got your face covered so I can't see your blackface make-up anymore," says Father. "That's something I think we can all care about."

"You're a racist."

"No one's a racist at 27,000 feet," Father says. "Everything's white!" He laughs. No one laughs with him.

I was just thinking that, William thinks. Which proves he's in me. My father is in my head. And now the air has gone white. The little black pieces of falling fate have turned white. The wind is drilling them into us. Is this the opposite of fate? All the things we weren't supposed to do, weren't supposed to be, weren't supposed to say, finally catching up to us before we reach the summit?

"This Hillary step here's a doozie," Father warns.

At last the summit is in sight. Or it would be if not for a white-out engulfing all the upper reaches of the world. They're on the exposed ridge in hurricane winds. They can't hear each other over the howl. They can't feel their extremities. They don't know if they're climbing, flying, or sliding. There's no one left to rescue them. When they left Camp 4 at midnight, the few other expeditions to make it that far took heed of the weather report and descended.

Mother is the first to leave. After an hour of sitting in the snow mumbling, she stands and steps out over the Kangshung Face. She soars through the infinite white to the City of Brians.

Later, Jennifer attempts to descend and freezes to death when she falls on the Hillary Step and breaks her leg. "Doozie" is the word she can't get out of her head as the rest of her shuts down.

Now it's just Father and William. They may be near the summit. They may be on the summit. They'll never know.

Father is saying some things that are lost in the wind. William has his hands around the Lucky Katana ice axe, the one he stole from Father. His grip is the only thing keeping him alive. The axe's heated handle never worked. It's not lucky, either.

Father seems to be urging him along. His slow, creaky gestures mean, *Almost there!*

William has the urge to say things back to him, things he should have said a long time ago. Somewhere, he wants to say, we all became people we weren't supposed to be. That's what I mean by the opposite of fate. We made each other say things and do things we never should have said and done. We prodded each other to become who we weren't. And we made each other into people we don't like. Because that way we didn't have to carry the burden of loving each other. It's easier not to. Just as it's always easier to be who you aren't.

William says nothing. He has no breath left for words, even if his father could hear them. Instead, he lifts the Lucky Katana, which is pretty well frozen to his hands.

He holds it out for his father, who has turned to yell something else that will be lost in the wind.

Here, thinks William. You can have it. You can do what you want with it. When I went back and got it, I decided it was for me, not you. But now I'm done with it. Thank you for leading me up so high so I could fall back into myself. Thank you for keeping our family flag in your pants. Thank you for everything.

That's all.

In the Shadow of the World's Greatest Monument to Love

When she was seventeen, a junior in high school, she had her first sexual experience with a thin young sophomore named Gordon. Gordon wore a peach-fuzz beatnik goatee, black t-shirts when his parents let him, and slicked back hair he arranged in the boys' bathroom before homeroom. Pale and pimply, he wrote songs and listened to bebop and when he whispered to her in sing-song rhythms, quoting poetry like he was performing, she loved him—or loved something—so much she wanted to cry.

Then she did cry, in the back seat of a ten-year-old Cadillac after he lifted her skirt, pinched aside the fabric between her legs, and finished off her virginity in four half-notes of his trumpet. She cried not because she hadn't protected herself, or because she'd mouthed a feeble no and he hadn't listened, but because something seemed to fall away afterward and reveal the world without her. How could anything matter again?

She stopped seeing Gordon. When he called at night, she left the phone on her bed and listened with her back against the pillows.

"Do you love me, babe? Do you love me back?" repeating himself until the words became a night bird's song.

The song stuck in her head through sixteen years of marriage to someone else. It popped into her thoughts at unexpected moments—during their vows, almost always during sex, and both times during labor. "Do you love me, babe? Do you love me back?" until it lost its beat and the words meant nothing at all.

Then, one morning three months after her fortieth birthday and eight months after she caught her husband cheating, she woke up wanting an answer to Gordon's sing-song question.

Her husband couldn't give her one.

In return, she gave him everything, including the kids. That shortened the battle. Four weeks later, he moved in with his girlfriend, who was younger and prettier and probably a better mother.

For a time, she cried and was full of regrets. While before she couldn't remember the good moments, now she couldn't remember the bad. Why had she left, really? What right did she have to expect anything better? It seemed she'd kicked herself out of her own home. And now she lived in a one-bedroom apartment beside a mini-mall and wouldn't go out at night for fear of thugs. What hope did she have of ever meeting someone else?

She thought she'd travel for a while, but on her slight hourly wage at the Golf Warehouse, where she sold clothes in the women's department, she barely had enough to pay bills. She ought to have asked for more in the divorce. She ought never to have asked for a divorce.

Months later, she did meet a man, a golfer who frequented the shop. He'd chatted with her, let on he was divorced, then asked if she played. She didn't; she didn't even like the clothes she sold.

But she was willing to learn.

The man, Frank, was much older, and charmingly timid. He played golf more for the setting than for the game, he admitted. He liked to find out-of-the-way courses, even if the greens were in sad shape. He had an extensive jazz collection and kept changing CDs in his Volvo as they drove to the public course on a Saturday.

"Do you like this?" he asked her. "How about this?"

Yes and yes. Three minutes later, he changed the music anyway.

She liked golf after all. It seemed a miracle when her slow, powerless swing shot the ball a hundred and fifty yards down the fairway. Strength and effort had little to do with it; the club had only to follow its ideal arc.

"You're a natural," said Frank, and after three weeks she almost bought it.

It turned out he wasn't divorced—just going through one— and his wife still lived at home. He was fifteen years older, too, and this worried her. What was she getting herself into? They could only meet afternoons and weekends at the golf course, sneaking around like kids.

One day on the driving range, Frank spoke about a travel show he'd seen the night before. There was a golf course near the Taj Mahal—can you imagine? Right in the shadow of the world's greatest monument to love. That was a quote from the show.

He got quiet for a minute, waiting, she thought later, for her to hit a good shot. When she did, he asked her if she wanted to take a trip with him to India and play the course. "It's only nine holes," he added.

His face colored. He wasn't joking.

She knew how it would look. Up till now, they'd only kissed and held hands. Her ex and her kids would laugh at her for dating an old man. They'd think she was desperate and pathetic. Still, dating Frank made her feel things she hadn't felt in many years. Maybe it was just the act of dating, and it mattered more what you did than who you did it with. She'd have saved herself a lot of grief if she'd recited that mantra years before.

"I'll go," she said.

Frank bought the tickets and reserved the room. They got their shots and passports together. He hoped the trip would help him celebrate his divorce and the beginning of a new life. Then the date for the divorce got pushed back, and Frank asked her to hold the tickets so his wife wouldn't find out. She knew what was coming.

Five days before the trip, Frank missed their Thursday golf date. He didn't call, and he didn't stop by the golf store to chat. When she tried to reach him, he didn't pick up.

She felt taken advantage of, like she'd accepted something less than she deserved out of politeness. Having reduced her wants, she found even those were too much. It was the mistake she'd made when she was young, when falling in love with a poet had tricked her into thinking her life would be more meaningful.

She went to India by herself.

On the long flight that passed through Frankfurt, she could sprawl out because the seat beside her was empty. She could look her worst and no one would care.

After the ordeal of the Delhi airport and the long bus ride to Agra, she laughed when she finally got to the hotel. Frank had reserved a room with twin beds. They'd have kissed with one foot on the floor, held hands across the nightstand in the dark. Like an old TV show.

When she showed up for her tee time at the Agra Golf Club the following day, the Taj Mahal's marble dome and minarets rose above the tree line in the distance, as promised. From this angle, they were pale in the too-bright morning sun. While beautiful, they weren't life-changing the way she'd hoped.

"The view is different late in the day," her caddy told her. "I could get you in."

The tall, young caddy had a peach-fuzz moustache and a wide, bright smile. A tangle of dark hair curled out from under his white cap and spiraled over his forehead. He kept a respectful distance and, after his bold first promise, spoke only when spoken to. Under his watchful eye, she played nervously and lost an historic number of balls in the trees and golden marshes. The whole trip seemed a waste. She'd expected to feel independent and worldly; instead, she felt disappointed and out of place.

Only a vague promise in her caddy's eyes kept her from quitting. When the round was over she asked him if she could try again tonight.

"At sunset," he said, "the Taj Mahal shows its colors. You will fall in love."

She smiled as she tipped him.

That evening he was waiting for her when the cab dropped her outside the club. He took her bags, and they bypassed the clubhouse for the first tee. He was right; on the Taj Mahal's marble skin, the pink and blue sky gave the illusion of life. To watch the colors change and move and slip into shadow was to fall in love with everything and nothing; it didn't matter which. Here was the poetry her young beatnik had promised and never delivered.

Her caddy waited until the third fairway to touch her. He came up behind her and placed his fingers on the waist of the golf skirt she'd bought with her employee discount.

He was half her age and smelled of cardamom and coriander and the thin, musky cologne he'd applied over a day's sweat. He led her off the fairway and under the spinning leaves of a Peepal tree, where he pinched open her waistband and bra and laid her down naked on a bed of moist brown leaves. She kept her eyes open and watched the play of light on the Taj Mahal's dome and spires, the great slow magic trick that made everything worthwhile.

"Do you love me?" asked the light.

"I love you back," she said.

Xenophilia

1

Seated at the quiet corner table he'd reserved by phone, the scientist studied the alien—the sad eyes deep behind high cheekbones, the pouty lips and tiny nose, the movement of its ears as it sipped from its water glass, the tilt of its chin as it caught his glance—and he concluded it looked remarkably like his ex-girlfriend. He didn't know for sure if those were eyes he was looking at, couldn't possibly say without x-rays (effects unknown) or God forbid an autopsy that the alien had a skeleton, could only guess that "face" was the correct term for the upper portion of the body across the table from him. Still, the likeness was obvious, and it surprised him that he hadn't noticed it before. The familiar features, he supposed, had only gradually taken shape, Magic Eye-like, out of the alien's untidy visage.

He'd chosen the restaurant on the hill, one of those converted farmhouses not advertised in the newspaper or listed in the phone book but always recommended to travelers and known simply as "the restaurant" to everyone in town—from the founders of the local country club, who had awarded the scientist an honorary membership after his Nobel Prize and who made the restaurant a part of their weekly meal plan; to the military officers and university faculty, who broke their budgets to eat there on special occasions; to the working villagers, whose frustrating dreams sometimes carried them to the threshold of the restaurant's walk-in but left them pining there for the dated bins of ambrosia just beyond their reach. This outing with the alien, while undeniably risky, seemed to him the essential next step in his studies. Here, in the security of the dark and woody ambiance, he could observe the alien in a setting more conducive to spontaneity. If not exactly home to the alien, the restaurant was at least more natural than the cold, sterile laboratory with its bubbling beakers and pulsing lights.

The scientist opened the oversized menu and the alien followed his lead, resting the menu on its lap, its tiny bulbous fingers curling around the leatherette, its chin lifting just slightly.

"Don't worry, I'll order for you," said the scientist, knowing that he need not say anything, that he only had to think it for the alien to understand, but enjoying anyway the primitive physicality of speech. The alien, economical in the extreme, said nothing, but continued to stare deeply and inscrutably at the scientist, who now felt a blush coming on.

He had taken his ex-girlfriend, a sociologist, to this same exquisitely overpriced restaurant once, to celebrate his Nobel privately. After the stiff academic galas, a quiet evening with his girlfriend seemed the best way to absorb the accolades, and also to ease himself back into his old lifestyle. They'd been dating for two months before he'd flown off to Stockholm, and he was anxious to pick up where they'd left off. She had never dated a scientist before and found his buzz cut and his horn-rimmed safety glasses "categorically masculine," his white lab coats "sultanesque."

Like the alien, she was quiet that night, too, sneaking glances at him over forkfuls of linguini-wrapped prawns, smiling cat-like and seductive.

She revealed her secret only after cappuccino and raspberry torte: she wanted to make love in the lab.

"There may be graduate assistants analyzing data," he protested. But that wasn't the real danger. "And there are chemicals," he added, "some of them explosive, some radioactive, some whose harmful agents we haven't yet isolated." But even those dangers, he knew, could not match the potentially cataclysmic mixture of science and love. The sociologist had proposed a new compound, something reckless and unstable, whose radiation, once released, might well be uncontainable.

But she had a way, and a look about her, and the scientist could not hatch a convincing excuse.

The lovemaking was operatic. Naked beneath their lab coats, they rolled across the stainless steel tables and Formica countertops as rows of gurgling beakers crashed to the floor. Bunsen burners ignited and doused and mysteriously re-ignited. Dangerous solutions pooled together on the linoleum, and harmful gasses billowed across the fluorescent ceiling panels. Condensation rained unchecked from the trembling copper coils. Switches were thrown and released, thrown and released, dials nudged to unacceptable settings, needles quivered into red zones, while the panels of multicolored lights pulsed out dangerous patterns and the warning tones glided up the scale, until finally, test tubes frothing over and noxious cumulus clouds raining blue ash, they were forced to pull the plugs and slink out coughing into the night.

In the morning, the university police suspected vandals,

local villagers provoked by rumors and by misleading TV exposés of scientific amorality. Security was stepped up, but that only increased the thrill. Night after night they returned, he nodding to the security guard and flashing his faculty I.D., she donning tinted glasses and tight hair and the thick and elusive accent of a distinguished foreign scientist. Once inside, her hair sprung and their lab coats unbuttoned, they abandoned themselves to their decadent routine: "Oh, Professor, you must come look!" and the science brought them together like a force of nature, "What is it, Professor?" her hand reaching back between the folds of his lab coat, "I think I've made a discovery," and he drew close, over her shoulder, the smell of her hair bursting and wild, a controlled experiment gone awry, and then, hands raising her lab coat in bunches, "Oh, Professor, you'll compromise the results," but with a sweep of his arm the gurgling beakers crashed to the floor and the stainless steel altars of science were theirs to defile.

But those crimes against science had to be paid for with trembling hands and ruined experiments. Mornings, he'd dial up the power on the control panel and be shaken by an ionized lungful of last night's air—her hair, her skin, her breath, their sex—and for the rest of the day his concentration tottered on a knife-sharp fulcrum of shame and desire. Even after he'd stopped returning the sociologist's calls, even after he'd been given the most absorbing scientific project of his career—the project of a lifetime, the study of a living alien—the ghosts of those carnal nights haunted him. He found himself more and more attracted to the alien, more and more casual about his laboratory decorum. And now that he recognized the creature's resemblance to his ex-girlfriend, he wasn't sure he could control himself.

2

The general had heard how the steaks here dissolved on the tongue like popsicles, sweet and bursting. He knew for a fact that his girlfriend would do the same at evening's end. The only question was whether she would go for the breathless claustrophobia of the M-1 Abrams ("But General, I've just locked onto an enemy tank!") or the apocalypse of the pock-marked artillery range ("But General, the troops need our support!").

But those pleasures ("Let them die!"), he reminded himself, were secondary to the task at hand: to monitor the scientist's increasingly suspicious relationship with the alien. He'd made it his special project, had code-named it "Hawkswoop," though the label appeared only on a single, thin, card-sized file folder in the lockbox he kept in his wife's hosiery drawer and was never muttered but in a close-lipped whisper in the dark. On a poorly lit street across from the university laboratory, he'd sit long nights in his baby-blue Mercury and listen through headphones to the one-way conversation between scientist and alien, imagining the scientist's movements and position by the volume and quality of his voice as it reached the bug. As the weeks passed and the scientist's diction tumbled slowly from lab jargon to prattle, the general understood that a breakthrough was imminent. One night there were long, nervous moments of silence, a phone picked up and re-cradled, a sigh, another attempt and a few numbers dialed, then, at last: "I'd like a reservation for two ..." And the general whispered his tight-lipped mantra all the way to the base: "The swooping hawk has fixed its prey ..."

"I recommend the prawns," said the sociologist, scanning her menu, "sir," she added, her voice thick with frisky mockery.

Tonight she wore a lieutenant's uniform, the skirt hemmed short, and the perversion fluttered on the general's tongue like a copped feel. He took a breath and tried to concentrate. Across the dusky ether of the cathedral-like dining room, the scientist chattered and smiled at the small, languorous, and human-like alien, whose tuberous neck hid behind a sporty red scarf. The scientist had clearly taken every precaution; in those clothes and in this lighting and in the peripheral vision of the self-absorbed patrons, the alien might well go unnoticed. Only a keen and interested observer would note that the rubbery arms lacked elbows, so that they bowed instead of bent, that the head quivered and pulsed like gelatin, and that the earholes tended to migrate. Those nubs on the scalp could easily be mistaken for a state-of-the-art hairdo.

Like so many other aliens, this one had crash-landed in the desert. But unlike the others, this alien miraculously survived. And then, incredibly, the President transferred sole, top-secret possession to this local scientist, whose recent Nobel had moved him to the top of the scientific pecking order—in the private sector, anyway. The President had said, in so many words, that the military could not be trusted to perform medical experiments within accepted ethical boundaries. But what did the President know about ethical boundaries? And what, in any case, were the ethics of alien testing? Hadn't the aliens abducted humans and performed painful and humiliating medical procedures? In the military's view—in *the general's* view—those were acts of war. It's never been proven, in any case, that aliens feel pain, or fear, or humiliation—that they feel anything at all. No, the only reason to restrain oneself around aliens was to protect oneself; self-abandonment was a weakness that aliens could exploit.

He'd seen their power, even in death. He'd lost three good officers, two of them top-notch military scientists, to the wiles of dead aliens. The first was a woman he'd personally appointed to lead the autopsy team. Before they opened the doughy corpse, she needed time to study its externals, she said, to understand what she could from its soft contours. She worked long hours in the lab, often by herself, and slept little. The general should have suspected something when he stopped by the lab on his way home one night and found his autopsy leader sponge-bathing the alien's fragile-looking, pearl-white body.

"Oh! Didn't hear you come in, sir!"

"The President's inquired about the delay. When are we a go?"

"Soon. I'm in the final phase of preparations, sir."

"Off the record, Miss Lundquist: are you in love with that alien?"

"No sir!" but the color came to her face, the sponge slopped onto the dead alien's thigh, and the general should have known.

One morning a week later they found her curled up under a sheet with the alien, weeping inconsolably, caressing the alien's leathery cheek. She had to be pried from it, one finger at a time. The room was sealed and quarantined, and the alien was frozen in a vault, its baby face veiled safely in rime.

Two more crash landings resulted in two more love-stricken officers, both of them still babbling and weeping in the psychiatric ward. And the President bestows on the private sector the first alien captured alive? It's unconscionably stupid, the general thought. It's blind.

"If he ever arrives, order me steak," he said, pushing his chair back.

The sociologist tossed him a limp salute.

The general made sure no one was looking. He paused at

the men's room door, slipped the tiny camera from under his tasseled epaulette, and snapped three shots of the alien and the scientist together, the scientist leaning close, fingers full of a dumpling appetizer, hesitating momentarily as he searched for the alien's mouth, laughing at his own awkwardness. He's doomed, thought the general. His brain is a marinated dumpling.

3

At the head of the posse, the deputy sheriff's torch burned brightest, the eye of a fiery snake winding up the hillside switchbacks. The restaurant's lights twinkled into view, still distant and fortress-like, but soon within their grasp. We are all torchbearers for the earth, he thought, and the idea filled him with the adrenaline his tired legs needed to set the pace.

"It's better this way," he told the man beside him, meaning *on foot*. "It shows them we're a grass-roots movement, that there's a groundswell of common rage."

"You got that right," said the man, slapping an oak cudgel against his palm.

"Just remember," said the deputy, "this is about love."

And it was, for the deputy sheriff loved the earth, both the idea and the thing itself. He loved the bigness of it. He loved the strength and permanence of it, but also the gentle curve of its horizon when it reached achingly for the setting sun. He loved its centrality and importance in the universe, neither of which was diminished by scientific models of this and that revolving around the other thing. He loved the soft blue sweetness of its breath. He loved the cool, moist soil, and when he came home from work each day he went straight to his garden and thrust his arms into the earth, cleansing himself of the rot and stench of humanity's crimes against itself. He loved the taste of the earth, too, not just its fruits but its dark and gritty flesh. The vegetables from his garden he ate unwashed, for to wash off the soil, he thought, was like washing away the dewy traces of love. And gardening, after all, was an act of love.

He loved the earth, which is why he took the trespasses of aliens personally. Their very existence threatened the earth's central position in the universe. Aliens demeaned her. And now, recently, they'd come calling, charming the earth with their bright little saucers and their babyfaces (he'd seen the video exposé), seducing her with technological panache, and threatening, in the end, to make of her a private satellite, just one more concubine in their orbiting harem. Others told him he was overreacting, that the evidence suggested the aliens intended only to study the earth. But those who did not love the earth could not be counted on to protect her. The evidence, he countered, suggested a long, lustful *leer* at the earth. Look at the shameful way they'd treated the abductees! Notice the suspicious nakedness of the little corpses pulled from downed saucers! No, the aliens' intentions were far from honorable. (And the apologists were quiet then. They knew; in their hearts they knew.)

Some joined the cause once they learned of the reckless collaboration between government and science. The deputy sheriff wouldn't have believed it himself if the security guard hadn't brought him into the lab one night. They stepped quietly into the back room, where the guard raised his finger and cocked his thumb at the prophetic image entangled on the gurney before them: a living alien resting cozily in the arms of a bare-chested scientist. He touched his holstered gun—but no, he reasoned, there is a better way. The aliens must be shown what they're up against. A crowd of angry humans must be assembled, and their fire and rage and collective strength must fill the viewscreens of every alien saucer and space station and planetary outpost until the message is loud and clear: we won't let her go without a fight.

Armed with torches and clubs, the posse had marched first to the college, which for so long had stood with folded arms in haughty disregard for the world. The scientists, after all, had never loved the earth. They belittled her with theories conjured from the test tubes and copper coils and the rest of the pornographic hardware they secreted in their noxious, windowless, linoleum-floored laboratories.

The scientist and his little green consort weren't there—the security guard thought he'd seen them drive off in the direction of the restaurant and an anonymous phone call confirmed it—but the angry mob sent a message, sweeping racks of colored chemicals to the floor, throwing beakers against the wall like Molotov cocktails, torching the control panels and melting the dials, burning notebooks and scholarly journals and other scientific smut, shouting and howling and clenching their fists in a climax of vengeance. The deputy had to pull himself together before he could collect the others.

Then they marched into the woods and up the hill, torches and fists raised to the hilltop fortress and the alien within. They climbed rocks and forded streams. Their shouts cleared away the nocturnal creatures before them, while a long trail of villagers scurried behind, some anxious to join the Cause, other curious to see the Effect.

"It's about love," repeated the deputy, the words directing his eyes to the hilltop, "love and a show of strength."

4

Even in the restaurant's dim light the sociologist recognized his thick safety glasses, his squarish coif, his weak jaw. And even now his classic features turned her on. The relationship was behind her, she told herself, and the feelings she had for him had moved on. She was having fun with the general now—well, not so much the general as *the military*. But in those last weeks with the scientist, there'd been something uncomfortably personal, some kind of sad, animal connection that transcended the idea, some kind of sticky Precambrian soup that flowed between them in the lab. It had scared them both. The general was just another uniform—granted, there were epaulettes—but a uniform just the same. And a uniform was simple and safe.

Now that the waiter had taken her order and her menu she watched with interest as the scientist grew more and more animated and giggly across the dining room. His date—a chilly, frumpy thing—sat stiffly, unresponsive but for the occasional wiggle of her ears—or were those lumps part of the scarf? What a homely outfit she wore—the scientist must have picked it out himself.

And when she tired of the military? When she'd completed her paper, "Womb with a View: Tanks and Gender in Today's Military"? When she'd presented it at the ASA convention and published it in the *Journal of Applied Sociology*? What then? She'd done politics. She'd done sports. She'd done television, radio, and film. What was there left to do? "When will you settle down?" her department chair had asked her time and again. She'd scoffed at him but knew, too, that she was getting a reputation in her field—many of the colleagues who'd once dubbed her "The Naughty One" and found her gonzo, interdisciplinary approach groundbreaking and courageous now called her a "nympho-sociologist" and found her studies showy, thin, and lacking rigor.

They were wrong, of course. The problem was her own failure to outdo herself. Revolutionary fervor is quickest to cool; only a more shocking revolution would quiet the critics and save her reputation. Then the doubts of many would ripen to affection.

So why hadn't she taken the next great leap? Had she grown smug? Had she grown frightened? She could ask the questions, at least. The answers would show in her actions, as they always did.

And then she had a thought that made her gag on her cabernet. She could not deny that her feelings for the scientist transcended the idea of *fucking his science*. What if she let herself love him?

Love was the final barrier—of course. Love was the nebulous realm of warm, fuzzy subjectivity—the very antithesis of academic discipline. Could she love him and still write a paper like "Safety Glasses and the Volatility of Desire" (work-in-progress) or "The Hermaphroditic Test Tube" (*American Sociology Review*, vol. 45 no. 1, spring 1995)? She had to admit some trepidation, for she was talking about a complete transformation of herself and her studies. Love, she knew, was often the kiss of death in her field; she'd seen the work of so many colleagues muddled by the vagaries of love. And loving the scientist—really loving him—meant, too, that the pleasures of the general's tanks and artillery ranges and tasseled epaulettes—of *fucking the military*—might forever be lost.

She focused again on the scientist, who had leaned in toward his date, smiling dumbly, both hands under the table, playing a secret game.

That did it!

She threw down her napkin and strode across the dining room.

"Bitch, you keep your slut knees clamped and your paws off my man!" and she slapped the scientist's date across the cheek, making a mental note of how cool and gummy that skin felt—a detail she might work into her paper, "Cat Fights and Doggie Bags: Public Displays by Jealous Women."

5

The manager had just scrutinized and okayed some foreign traveler's checks when the parking attendant rushed into her tidy, wood-paneled office with news of an approaching mob.

"PETA again?" she asked, shaking her head as she returned the checks to the patient waiter. "Just make sure he signs the back," she told him. The local PETA chapter had threatened her over the phone and had once demonstrated in her driveway. They believed the rumors, apparently started by some disgruntled employee, that the restaurant served live monkeys in its banquet room for guests to club to death and eat.

"I don't think PETA would carry torches through the woods," volunteered the attendant. "Threat of habitat destruction."

"Torches?" she asked, recognizing another daily threat to the thin stability she'd built from the wreckage of her divorce. Breathe, she thought, getting up slowly. Focus on your attitude. "You sure those aren't just deer with flaming antlers?"

The attendant shrugged.

"That was a joke," she said, breathing again.

The manager left her office and stepped out into the crisp night air just in time to see the torches bob over the rocks like flaming marionettes. And then she saw the arms that held them, and then the faces, and then, when they had fanned out in a semicircle in front of her, her ex-husband stepped forward. She swallowed, knowing this would be her greatest test yet. The torchlight showed off the ruddy complexion on one side of his face, left the other side darkened in mystery.

"Don't make a scene," she said instinctively.

"Honey," said the deputy, "this is not a social call."

"Oh," she said, fists clenched tight to keep her in the moment. "I thought you'd brought the bowling league in for tea."

"Let's burn it down!" shouted a man in the crowd. "They're killing monkeys in there!"

"Shut up!" yelled the manager. "There's never been a monkey within a mile of here. Until now," she added.

"You hear her!" the man responded. "There *are* monkeys!"

"Shut up!" said the deputy. "That's not why we're here."

His voice was flat and resolute, as it was in their last months together, when the marriage had crumbled and he'd clearly given up, working late hours and then coming home to a pup tent he'd pitched in their garden. No matter how loudly she screamed, how many vases she broke, how many times she threatened to kill herself, he never once raised his voice or lost control. And that only made her want to scream louder, throw harder, show him a razor blade that she almost intended to use.

"Then why?" she asked him now. "Are you here to burn the place down? Is this part of your scorched earth divorce policy?"

"We're here for the alien," he said gravely.

She looked confused, then offended. She folded her arms self-consciously. "The kitchen staff all have their green cards," she said. "I take no chances."

"I'm talking about a guest," he said.

She laughed, releasing the tension and spraying him, she noticed, with dots of saliva. "The little foreigner? He seems harmless enough."

"He's a threat to all we hold dear," said the deputy.

"His traveler's checks are good," she said. "I'll vouch for that."

"Honey, I'm asking you on a personal level," he said, covering his badge with three fingers. "Will you bring him to us?"

His oath would have seemed comical if he weren't backed by dozens of glowering torches and strange, flickering faces. "You aren't going to hurt him," she said. "You're just going to deport him or something, right?"

"That's right, honey. We aren't going to do to him what he's done to so many of us. We're humans," he said, proud of the fact.

Their eyes locked for a moment, his gaze almost tender, until she looked away in fear. She couldn't let him do it again. Her life had finally stabilized. She had to let go.

"Let's burn it!" shouted the man in the crowd, and now a few others echoed his desire.

"As soon as he's finished his cappuccino," she told the deputy.

"Soon," he said.

"You'll wait," she said, "like I used to," and she spun and walked back into the restaurant, her steps decisive and her nails digging into her palm.

She closed and locked the office door behind her, pulled an egg timer from the top drawer of her desk, and cried for exactly three minutes. Then she returned to the dining room.

6

"Another cappuccino," the foreigner called to the waiter, who paid no attention because he was busy breaking up a fight between two women. What the damn kind of place is this? he thought.

The foreigner used to receive prompt service and special attention wherever he traveled. That was when he had a country to love and when his love of country carried him to the upper echelon of international diplomacy. People respected him ("Can we getting you more béarnaise sauce, sir?" "Might you honor us by acceptance of a cappuccino gift, sir?"), and he floated with natural grace in the champagne of their diligent attendance (an urbane nod of the head, bestowing a courteous acceptance).

Then his country splintered, and the ennobled idea of his country crumbled into the basest kind of group attachments—religion, ethnicity, class, proximity—and for him the pride of patriotism, the hand-over-heart reverence and the high-stepping exaltation, was lost forever. Buildings, flags, constitutions, and bridges burned, and suddenly, in mid-diplomacy, the champagne stopped bubbling and the viewing stand collapsed and in the wreckage of his once-noble devotion a tuxedoed waiter stepped forward with an overlong leatherette portfolio: "Your check, sir."

And now, a diplomat without a country, he wandered aimlessly from nation to nation and town to town, seeking out former haunts and cronies, hoping to recapture some of the glory—the velvet salons, the kitchen sink debates, the state dinners, the military parades—but most of the cronies no longer cared for his company, and most of the official state functions were now closed to him, and the white-gloved service revealed itself as just another paid performance that he could no longer afford. Which is how he ended up in restaurants like this—cock-a-hoop roadhouse diners staffed by pretentious bumpkins and patronized by belligerent women. Look at the one trying to strangle the other with the other's scarf! America, he thought, always was I saying a doomed country was.

"Yes, another cappuccino for which I was asking," he told the red-eyed woman who now approached his table.

"Sir, you'll have to come with me," she said.

"But I am not completed yet," he told her sharply.

She touched his arm in an offensively familiar manner. "There are people outside who need to see you."

There were two possibilities: either the intelligence splinter from his old country had cornered him for erasure, or some of his old diplomatic cronies had finally agreed to meet him. Either way, he was embarrassed to be found here.

As the woman rudely pulled him up by the arm, he thought he heard her say, "Forget the check."

At least there was that.

7

The mob's will had become one, and their fears fueled their passions. Their grumbles became shouts, and their shouts turned to chants, and the chants got crafted into a call-and-response:

"What do we want?"

"A-li-en!"

"How do we want it?"

"To go!"

Even the deputy sheriff joined in. At first, they laughed like collegiate tailgaters at their own cleverness, but as their impatience grew the song tightened into a sharp rhythm, and the blood thumped in their chests and their voices shrilled and their fears were overcome by lust. The nocturnal animals, who had edged up the hill out of curiosity, now scampered back to their dens in fear.

The mob edged closer to the double doors, fists, torches, and cudgels thrusting skyward, demanding satisfaction with their shouts and chants. Their distorted, angry faces glared in the torchlight, and the building trembled with their stomps.

Then, as if on cue, the heavy wooden doors split open and the foreigner popped out with a quick shove.

"What is this?" he seemed to mouth, but it was too late even to ask. The crowd converged, screeching through clenched teeth, their eyes wide with mindless lust.

The lawlessness! they thought. But when they grabbed the creature's pinstriped lapels, their fists thought for them, bunching the fabric and strangling it in the name of the earth, though at that moment even the noble cause slipped their collective mind. They twisted and tore the fabric, hissing madly, gathering strength from the frenzy around them. They wanted to laugh and kill all at once.

To the extent they thought, they now thought only, Yes . . . yes.

And the foreigner looked up at them, eyes wide with terror, forearms offering meager protection, oiled hair spiking in disarray, bushy mustache stained with blood and mucous, split lips quivering, unable to speak. How could this be? he wanted to think. To die for no country, to give one's life for no cause. The indignity! The humiliation! The senselessness! I cannot abide it, he wanted to say, or at least to think, yet the words could not form themselves out of the commotion of pain.

Just as he felt himself losing consciousness, he took a last look at his attackers and saw the deputy sheriff staring in slack-jawed astonishment at his own fists.

"It's blood!" shouted the deputy in a voice so shocked that it roared above even the foreigner's agonized screams and cut off the mob's fury all at once.

"It's human blood!" he said, still amazed, raising his stained fists for everyone to see.

And the foreigner, mouth open and drooling bubbles of blood, breath wheezing and hot, collected himself in the momentary silence and finally crafted a thought: No damn shit.

8

The parking attendant did as he was told, helping the manager to evacuate guests out the back door. "No need to panic," the manager kept saying, which translated as, "Pay your bills first." But when the guests tuned in to the shouts and the noisy scuffle outside, they panicked. Food was left uneaten and checks unpaid, chairs got kicked over, wine spilled on the carpet. And the staff panicked, too: a busboy dumped his tub outside the kitchen door, and cooks and dishwashers tripped over it, kicking its contents across the room.

The parking attendant did as he was told, distributing the keys quickly to the guests, opening doors when he could, accepting tips when offered, but thinking all the while, The light of justice will shine, and as the last guests wheeled away he grabbed his backpack out of the car and slipped unnoticed back into the restaurant. He rolled aside fallen tables, kicked a martini glass through the uprights of a toppled chair, then paused before the kitchen door, still swinging in and out, revealing the sauces still flaming on the burners, the soufflés beginning to collapse, the steaks now charring on the grill.

The kitchen was the inner sanctum of the evil that had thus far evaded justice. It had always been off limits to him. But now the light will shine, he thought, unzipping his backpack and pulling forth the video camera and flashlight that PETA had presented him when he'd secured a job in the restaurant.

It had taken months of demeaning labor, but tonight his patience would pay off. He would rip out the very heart of this evil and raise it to the light of justice.

He held the camera to his eye; he wanted to see it as the world would see it—the startled, shivering monkeys cowering from the light, their experience—yes experience, because monkeys think, monkeys learn—telling them that another one of them was doomed to have his neck clasped between the leaves of a table and his head malleted by sportive carnivores, his brains forked into the salivating mouths of his devourers. "What flavor!" the guests would say. "They must forcefeed them a spicy marinade!"

He pushed open the door and panned across the flaming steaks and saucepans, zoomed in on a half-cooked T-bone melting on the floor in a pool of its own pink juices, then zoomed out and tracked through the wreckage toward the stainless door of the walk-in. The staff had not only left the door unlocked but also cracked open, and the cold mist curled around the edges and condensed into droplets on the door's bright surface. And now he heard the noises, too—the startled little grunts and gasps of their suffering, their fear of the light and the fate awaiting them. "No need to fear this light, little friends," he said aloud, clicking on his flashlight, aware that at this moment his eye was the world's eye, his voice the world's voice, and his light the light of justice. "This is the light of justice," he said, just to be certain his thoughts were the world's thoughts, too.

At last he reached out and grabbed the cold, wet edge of the steel door and drew it open slowly, dramatically, his light at the ready for all the world to see. The grunts and gasps grew louder and clearer, and then—because he, like all the world, could no longer stand the suspense—he yanked open the door and shined his light inside at the quivering white buttocks and splayed legs of human copulation. The light and the camera panned up until the man craned his neck around and met the lens through thick, horn-rimmed glasses, and the woman leaned up on her elbows and shouted, "Don't worry, Professor, our love's no secret anymore!" The man ripped off his glasses, flung them into an open food bin, then resumed his thrusting.

The animals, the world wanted to think. But the world could not quite shape a thought out of the white noise of its fascination, and it could not turn its eyes away.

9

I have impressed even myself, the general thought. He had let the confusion of the rioting villagers work to his advantage, sweeping the alien's soft body into his arms and dashing out the door with the panicked diners—"Excuse me! Excuse me! My wife needs a doctor!"—pushing through the genteel throngs to his baby-blue Mercury and depositing the docile alien onto the soft vinyl. He tore down the hill and took the back road that led to the base. The crescent moon hung sleepily above the mountains, and he opened his vent to let in the cool desert air. He took a deep breath, then looked over at the alien beside him, seatbelt fastened, quirky features softened by starlight and the glow of the dash. He couldn't tell for sure if the alien was looking at him, didn't know for sure that aliens "looked" at anything.

"Must get lonely for you so far from home," he said, immediately regretting the stupidity of talking to an alien, but feeling thoroughly intoxicated by the success of Operation Hawkswoop.

In the silence, he planned his next step: he would take the alien to his private M-1 Abrams and guard it personally until he could make radio contact with the right people, the scientists on his own team, ones who could keep their mouths shut and their hands above the table, ones whose dedication to the military took precedence over their dedication to science or to other such perversions.

"You'll be safe with me," he said again, smiling now at his embarrassing adolescent vanity. He smoothed one of his graying sideburns, then laughed aloud.

"You must think me a fool," he said, shaking his head, blushing, "but I'm not always this way . . ."

10

The alien smiled at the general's words and especially the general's thoughts, though the general could not see the smile, hidden as it was in the alien's clasped palms.

We're much the same, thought the alien. We live for love and die for lust.

In the distance, a flaming saucer arced romantically across the desert sky toward a fateful union with the earth. Inside, its alien pilot stared blankly at the viewscreen, transfixed by the primitive copulation it showed, the strange abandonment of two naked humans as they pulled food bins off the shelves of a walk-in freezer and soiled themselves in a strange primordial recipe. Yes, thought the pilot, oblivious to flames and impending doom. Yes.

Coward

When he was six, his father held a knife to his throat and threatened to kill him if he ever touched his LPs again. Later, in the war, he captured a VC and held a knife to the man's throat in the same way his father had held a knife to his. "I'll kill you," he told the man. "If you ever so much as…" and he couldn't think of what to say next. But realizing the man spoke no English he said it anyway: "I'll kill you if you ever mess with my records." He laughed until his jaw ached. Then he released the man, kicked him in the groin, and ran back to camp, where he sat on his cot and took the knife to the toes of his left foot, stretching them out and sawing them off one through five. His CO called him a coward and assured him a dishonorable discharge. On the plane home, he kept turning over in his mind the word coward. He'd lost the sense of its meaning.

Back before the war, during his one year in college, he'd DJed for the college radio station on the night shift. He geared his show toward late-night lovers and developed a following for the risqué tunes he played, becoming known on campus as the Pantydropper. A local minister overheard this and decided one night to drive through campus and listen to the college radio station. The minister's ears burned with righteous indignation, and the next day he mounted a campaign to shut down the college station unless it cleaned up its act. The station's faculty advisor promptly removed him, and while a few students complained about the decision in the campus newspaper, they did it mainly in jest: "Report: Panties Up All Over Campus."

Later, when he quit school, the campus protesting came in earnest over the war, and he felt ashamed—not for failing to stand up for himself at the station but for having indulged in adolescent mischief while people his age were dying overseas. He did what he thought was honorable: he joined the army.

•

When he was nine, his father finally left home for good. For a year after that, he and his mother lived in fear that his father might return home one night, as he had before, drunk and angry, waving a gun or a knife. Then one day a policeman came to the door and reported that his father had killed himself just two miles away at the riverfront. The policeman handed over the contents of his father's pockets—a photograph and a note—which, as far as anyone could tell, were the only belongings he had. The photograph was the family portrait they'd had done at the Montgomery Ward, his mother and father standing together and smiling, his father's thick fingers curled over his son's shoulder blade. The note was not addressed to his son by name but its target was clear anyway. In the split second before his mother crumpled it up, he read the deliberate letters written by an unsteady hand: *Don't be weak your whole life.* He never let on that he'd seen it.

The dishonorable discharge kept him from landing a job. The better employers were wary of Vietnam vets. They'd heard some were drug users, others killers. They wanted to see his discharge papers for reassurance. Eventually he quit applying and for a while tried to involve himself with the antiwar movement. He worked at KPFA in Berkeley in exchange for food and lived with two free-love lesbians in a room above College Street. They invited him to watch. "But if you ever so much as touch either one of us, you're back on the street," said the taller one. He couldn't help himself with the shorter one. She let him.

After, feeling tender toward her, he let on that he'd fought overseas. Only now, being with her, did he truly feel he was on his way home, he said. Later, she felt guilty and told her partner everything.

Perhaps he shouldn't have revealed his deformed foot; perhaps he should have kept his socks on. The partner spit at him and kicked him out, and someone at the radio station must have heard because they let him go without an explanation.

He decided he was always trying to make up for his earlier failures. Time to make a clean start. He cut his hair and drove east. He wrote his mother for money and used it to enroll in college, just as he said he would. He hadn't seen his mother in years, but they still kept in touch from time to time by mail. Her letters always sounded stiff because she didn't use contractions; he translated them in his head to the voice he remembered. She asked him questions and said little about herself except to end each letter, "I am fine, and I know you will be, too. Your loving mother, Doris." Though he knew it was coming, every time he reached this last line he felt like crying anyway. It was something she used to say to him when his father acted up. Sometimes she'd say it with a bruised face and tears streaking her cheeks. "I'm fine," she said, "and I know you will be, too."

Maybe he would be. He was taking business classes, having what he thought of as "normal" conversations with people he'd never imagined talking to before—people with family money and traditional values. As far as they knew, he was one of them. He didn't let on that he'd been in the war; he said only that he'd worked in his father's business for a time, then decided to cut out on his own, and most were impressed by that. He didn't mind being a faker and a liar if that's what it took to fit in.

He'd had some practice in the army, after all. He'd had to fake his own bravery, for one. And lie about the things he'd do or the things he'd done. He wasn't alone; the only ones not faking were the Certifiably Insane. The CI had been there too long; they'd forgotten it was all a lie. When the CI killed a Viet Cong, they meant it. All *he* could do when the time came was to borrow a line from his dad and then laugh about it.

To survive in business, he just had to keep from laughing, he thought.

•

The night his father held a knife to his throat, a laugh might have killed him. Yet he'd almost laughed anyway. He didn't know what LPs were. They were all over the floor at his knees, and he knew them only as records. What was an LP? In his dad's thick, gin-soaked voice, it came out as "help-please": "I'll kill you if you ever touch my help-please again."

It didn't make sense. On rare occasions, his dad came home not angry but silly—so silly he seemed to think it was a contest to out-do his small son—and maybe this was one of those times. But no, he knew better. There was a knife at his throat, and the knife meant business even if his dad didn't. If his throat convulsed, the blade would dig in.

He wanted to laugh. He wanted to swallow. He couldn't do either, not even when his father swatted his head aside like a basketball so he fell onto the records and cracked one.

•

He kept himself together and got his degree. When his mother came to the graduation ceremony, they hugged and cried. They hadn't seen each other in eight years. At fifty-five, she looked like a scared bobbing head swept in a strong current. She lived alone and had her routines.

"War injury," he told her when she asked about his limp, and that was enough to keep her from asking again.

When he marched, and brought his diploma back to her as a gift, she told him how proud she was.

"I knew you'd be fine," she said, and it didn't matter to him that she was probably lying, because even if her thin thread of hope had fallen slack at times, he'd drawn it tight around his diploma now like a ribbon.

"You're right," he said. "You always were."

He had a job waiting for him at a media company that was busy buying up radio stations around the country. He'd work for a marketing team—the company was big into teams, and he was to call his boss his "team leader."

The team leader was firm but chummy, an ex-marine who shook his hand hard and gripped his shoulder as he showed him around the first day. This made him more nervous. When his team was called out into the aisle to meet the new guy, the leader told a bawdy joke, something to break the ice, a little story about a Vietnam vet in bed with Jane Fonda.

Everyone around him laughed, and when he swallowed and opened his mouth, just to try it, he found he could laugh, too, just as long and loud as the others.

Wind and Rain

First let me tell you about the rain, Louis.

Last night it started to rain when I walked home from the hospital. I didn't even notice it for a while because it was thin and slow. Then the mist thickened and began to roll over me. A few drops ran down my cheek. By the time I came out of the liquor store, the rain was full and steady and the whole world looked shut down and closed up.

When it rains like that I think about the cop and what the cop said in his report. He said maybe it was the rain that made him believe he saw a gun in there. You remember what was in there? I do. When I went and claimed your car from the police, the first thing I did was search through the glove compartment. There was an owner's manual for the wrong model—for a Monte Carlo instead of Grand Prix. There were a few notes from Lila. I read them, hope you don't mind. *Baby, Meet you here at 3, Love, Baby.* None worth keeping; you probably just put them there to put them somewhere. There were a couple of paper clips in there. A broken pencil. A mileage log from the previous owner. Gum. Tic-tacs. A plastic bag with cookie crumbs. Your driver's license.

How could he mistake any of that for a gun? Can the rain change things that way?

Last night I sat on my bed and watched the rain. At the liquor store I'd gotten beer and Old Crow. I poured some of the Old Crow into my flask to take to work today. Then I took a big swig and felt it warm me. Mom doesn't like me drinking in the house, but she works cleaning offices now, doesn't get back until two a.m. I leaned back against the wall and looked at the rain. It was hard and steady, just the kind of rain the cop was looking through. I tried to test my eyes, to see things the way that cop did. I looked across the street and I could see the big cracks in Mr. Cullen's driveway, the water streaming through those cracks and over the lumpy places where he'd tried to repair them. I could see the car under the carport and could tell it was a Dodge Diplomat even though I couldn't make out the badge on the trunk. I could tell it was in pretty good shape for a car that old. I could see the striped awning over Cullen's living room window. There are eighteen stripes, and the water ran off each one. I could see through the living room, too, where the curtains weren't pulled together. Cullen was in his chair, watching TV. I couldn't tell what show, but there was lots of action and quick scene changes. An adventure show, maybe, or a kung fu movie. Next to Cullen was a lamp on a table, and on the table was something I couldn't see so well. I thought maybe it was an ashtray. I stared at it for a minute and tried to imagine it was a gun. I squinted my eyes a little. I focused on different parts of it and tried to reshape it in my mind. It was no gun. Even if I could make it look like one, I knew Cullen would not have a gun there. And anyone who knows you knows that you would not keep a gun in your car.

I don't ever imagine things in the rain. It's under the bright lights here that I sometimes have problems. Sometimes when I'm here I think I see things that later I know I didn't. I think I see your fingers move. I think I see your eyes start to open, or your lips start to say something. I'll see it out of the corner of my eye and then I'll put down my magazine and move my face right up next to your plastic mask and I'll try to see it again. And sometimes I think I do. Then I'm not sure. I remind myself that the doctors say there's no way.

There's all that junk I put inside me, Louis. The beer and the Old Crow. That kind of rain can cloud up your eyes from the inside.

Maybe the cop really thought he saw something and that's why he fired his gun. Later, when he got back to work after his suspension, he should've known he was wrong. But maybe he'd already stopped thinking about it.

It was raining, and I saw everything clearly. I still do. And I think you do, too. Your eyes aren't open, but you're not dead, so you must see something. Do you still see the rain that night, streaking the windshield and dulling the glow of the streetlights? Maybe you're still looking into the glove compartment, watching your hand grab the license, your frozen picture coming into view. I hope that's all you see. I hope you don't see that cop out of the corner of your eye, raising the gun toward your head. I hope you don't see the flash.

I told you once you ought to keep your real license in your wallet. What if a cop comes up on the street? But you said a cop can't ask you for your license if you're not in a car. You kept the fake license in your wallet just so you could go to bars with me, your big brother. And then you put the real license in your glove compartment. It's still there. I see it.

I see the cop following us after we leave the bar. I'm looking over the seat and I'm seeing his lights right behind you. It's raining pretty hard and maybe you should be driving slower, but that cop shouldn't be on your tail like that. He's trying to scare you, Louis. I see that now. I see the cop's headlights, and I see his grille, the grille of a Caprice Classic. I see the big, wide hood. The wipers going. You know what else? I see his face, too. Maybe there was a little light coming from his radio or something. But there it is. His big wire-rims. His pocked cheeks. I see him twenty years ago, too, a high school kid who doesn't fit in. Too much acne. Never got used to the way his own voice sounded after it changed. I see him reaching up to give a little siren blast. He likes the siren a lot better than his voice, though he's never gotten used to that, either.

I see you walking back to him in the rain. He shines his spotlight on you. You lean over trying to hear him in the rain, and your shirt clings to your skin. The water drips off your hair, your nose, your chin. You reach for your back pocket. Then you remember.

What's up? I ask when you climb back in the car.

I forgot my damn license.

I told you.

The cop has followed you back. He's shining his flashlight around inside. On your eyes, on me, on the back seat, then back to your eyes.

You lose something? you ask him.

That was a dumb thing to say, Louis. I know you can see all right, but you aren't thinking clearly.

The cop has on a hooded slicker. The rain is loud as it bounces off his hood. There are a few drops of rain on his glasses. Maybe those drops are right in front of his eyes. There are drops on the face of his flashlight, too, and maybe that changes the way things look to him. It's raining harder, now. Everything is splashing and making noise. The street and the roof of the car and the cop's slicker and the cop's flashlight. Like a machine grinding to a stop. In this kind of rain, most people sit in their houses and wait for it to end. They don't think anything that happens out in the rain can make any difference. They wait it out. Then they start their lives again. Maybe the cop thinks that, too. Nothing that happens now is going to count. When the rain stops and the water flows down into the street drains, anything that happens out here is going to flow with it.

We know better. The rain stays with us, and everything that happened in the rain happens again and again.

He said he saw something. Can a license ever look like a gun? Even with rain on your glasses and on the face of your flashlight?

Let me see your license.

You almost say something. Then I see your hand in front of my knees. The glove compartment is open. The flashlight beam is there. You feel around for just a second. You touch the notes from Lila. The owner's manual for the wrong model. The broken pencil. You feel your license.

Then everything stops. The rain falls over the car and stops everything inside it. The hand touching the license. The gun rising and flashing. Your head falling to my knee. My hand jerking up against the window. A dark streak on the window, not washing away in the rain. I'm thinking, What is that? What is it? The same thought the cop might have asked himself a second earlier. You could have answered it for him, Louis.

All of these things are now one moment, and that moment

is stuck inside the rain that falls in us both. Everything's clear in there. I wonder if the cop ever sees it, too. Or does the cop still see the gun that isn't there? Does he wonder what it's like to be you, Louis, stuck inside one rainstorm and always living just that one moment, not remembering anything before or after, nothing ever changing?

I know you know all this, Louis. You don't need me to tell you what you see. But in all the times I've come here, I've never talked to you about it. Not once. And when I looked out at the rain last night with the Old Crow warming inside me, I thought maybe you'd like to know that I see it, too. Part of the time I'm out here seeing other things, but most of the time I've been in the rain with you, and I thought you might want to know that.

The rain is why you're here, Louis. It's why I've been coming here up till now, even when everyone else began to fall away into their old lives. They went back in their homes to wait it out. We stayed out in the rain. For you it never stops. But I've been thinking about other things, too, and last night I started to put them together. I thought you'd want to know what I've been thinking. It's been so long since I said anything to you, Louis. I didn't think it would change anything. But now I'm going to tell you everything I know. It's not much, but it's something. You already know about the rain. Now I'm going to tell you about the wind.

A week after the shooting, I was back to work on the golf course. The superintendent said he was going to give me busy work for a while, stuff to take my mind off it. The irrigation man would fill in as his assistant. Any paperwork could wait. This went on for a few weeks, and I was beginning to think I'd lost my position. I didn't say anything, though.

One day I was out raking leaves. There was no wind that day, but there had been the night before, and the wind had blown pine needles and avocado leaves all over the greens. I was working ahead of the greens-mower, Enrique, clearing the leaves off so he could mow the greens evenly. Three-sixteenths of an inch all over. It was mid-afternoon, hot and still. I had to rake because the blower wasn't working.

The sweat rolled down my neck and got soaked up by my work shirt. There were only a few golfers around. Quiet day. Only the sound of Enrique's mower one or two holes back, the sound of my rake.

I'd been raking all day, not even stopping for lunch, so I could keep ahead of Enrique. I was doing the same kind of work I started doing there six years ago, and that was getting me worried. That irrigation guy was good friends with the superintendent. They both had agronomy degrees from Gainesville. Here I was doing the work of a high school kid. No offense, Louis, but I'd already been through it. I didn't want to do it again. I'm older. I've got experience.

My arms and back ached from the raking. I was thinking about my job. I was thinking about you. I didn't bring a flask to work then, but I'd had plenty the night before and plenty in the morning. It was still with me. My head wasn't right.

It was quiet and hot and then something came out of the clear sky and knocked me in the head. I remember the sound of it, like the crack of a baseball bat. And the echoes in my blood that made it seem for a second all my veins would explode at once. All I could hear was the crack and it was everywhere, and then it was only in one small spot on my head. I rubbed the tears out of my eyes and saw I'd dropped the rake. I reached up and felt my head. It seemed to swell under my hand. It throbbed, and the blood warmed my fingertips.

My eyes still closed, I heard an electric cart whir up beside me, right next to the collar of the green. Someone clicked on the brake lock. I blinked a few times and looked up. There were two old men there, and they were staring at me like I was something in the way of their golf game. Something they had to check the rule book about. A divot that hadn't been repaired or a tree limb in the way of their backswing.

Then the man stood up next to the cart and turned toward his friend behind the wheel. You ought to thank him, he said. His head kept your ball from slicing into the trees.

They both laughed.

That's when I first started to think about the wind.

Do you remember when I started work on the golf course? You were only a kid. You said, How do you play that game? I tried to explain it then, but I didn't know all that much about it myself. Now I do.

Here's how you play it, Louis. First you go into the woods and yank out most of the trees. Then you bring in truckloads of grass from Kentucky or Bermuda or somewhere else and you carpet over the space you cleared. Next you get your mowers out and you mow the grass again and again until it's so short you can't even call it grass anymore. You call it green, because you can't tell it's anything else. Some of it you call fairway, which sounds a lot like freeway, which is what they ought to call it, because it's smooth and wide and the golfers drive up and down it in their little cars, weaving side to side like they own the road. Once you've got all the grass in and you've mowed it down to its color, then you build a few little mounds and you fill them in with sand, and they're like little deserts that get in your way, except you rake them real smooth so they're more like the beach in front of the Breakers Hotel. Once everything's been torn out and sodded and raked and mowed, then you finally get to knock a little white ball around until it falls into a cup. And if it takes you a long time to do it, it's nobody's fault but your own, because everything's been cleared out and mowed down for you. Everything's exact. Only the wind can change where your ball goes. If there's no wind, then you've got no excuse. If you hit the ball and it curves, it's only because you didn't hit it right, and if you hit the ball and it lands on somebody's head, it's because that's where you aimed it.

This is what I decided was true with those two old golfers standing right in front of me, my head throbbing, and blood on my fingertips. I thought, Any excuse they've got has been cleared out and raked up and mowed away. The grass is exact and the fairways are wide open. The only thing left is the wind, and there was no wind. If there'd been wind and the guy had taken the same shot, the ball would have sailed over my head or maybe a little to the right and I wouldn't have thought any more about it. If the guy had taken a different shot and the wind had pushed it into my head, the guy would have that excuse. But there was no wind. The guy had aimed the shot exactly at my head, and once he'd struck the ball, there was nothing to make it change its course.

It was all clear to me as I watched them smile at each other. The ball was sitting on the collar of the green between me and them. My head was bleeding. I took a step and picked up the ball, then walked over to the man who'd spoken, grabbed him by the back of his white hair, and jammed the ball through his teeth. When the ball fell to the grass, it was spotted with blood.

The board of directors couldn't understand it. I hadn't even hit the man who'd swung the club. I'd hit his friend. I don't know why I hit his friend; it didn't seem to matter. It still doesn't.

The board called in the superintendent and asked him about it, and the superintendent told me he couldn't answer them. He explained my situation to them. They said they understood, but that they couldn't keep an employee who endangers the golfers, especially ones who've done nothing wrong.

I said, So if I'd hit the other guy, I could've kept my job?

The superintendent shook his head.

Because I can still go hit him.

The superintendent just stared.

When I walked out of there for the last time, I thought, if there'd been a breeze everything would be different. None of this would have happened.

Bad things happen where there's no wind, Louis. I know that now. You know something? There was no breeze that night in the rain. Can you see that? There's lots of rain and I guess you can call it a storm. But there's no wind at all. I know that because I see how the rain comes straight down. It bounces off the top of the cop's slicker, off the top of his flashlight, off the top of his gun. Exactly off the top.

I left my job knowing something about the wind. I was going to learn more.

I never told you any of this before. I never thought it would matter. Now I have to. I have to tell you everything.

After I left the golf course, I looked around for a while, but I had to take something quick. This room you've got isn't cheap, and Mom doesn't make nearly enough cleaning offices. I had to have something. There was this man down at the City Sanitation who remembered Dad. Dad was the first man he'd hired, he said. And somehow he'd heard about what happened to you. Newspapers, maybe. He sent a note to Mom, and Mom told me about him. It was nice of him to remember, she said.

I didn't want to talk to him, but I had to, and he offered me a job loading garbage. I know you've done better, he said. But your father managed it for a long time and he never complained. He was a good man, he said.

I remember the first time I smelled Dad. You were just a baby, and I'd been blowing up balloons all day and throwing them into your playpen. I remember the taste and the smell of those balloons. Like a hospital, clean and dry.

By the time Dad came home, I was out of breath and a little dizzy. I could still smell the clean smell of the balloons until Dad crouched down next to me. Then I smelled him. I'd never smelled him before. I moved my face away and frowned. Dad didn't say anything, but he might have noticed because he left the room then to take a shower. I tried to make an animal out of the balloon he'd blown up for me. It popped in my hands and I smelled him again.

Once I noticed that smell, I couldn't forget it even when I tried. Even when Dad took a shower, I smelled it. When I was almost old enough to start working myself I thought, I never want to smell like that. I didn't mind the smells on the golf course—the grass, the machines, even the chemicals. All those things were better than the smell of someone else's garbage.

I never asked you, Louis. Did you ever smell Dad that way? I smelled it on him even when he lay in this same hospital breathing through a tube like you. We both went to see him, and I wondered then if you smelled him, too. But I couldn't ask. Now I wonder if you can smell me. For the last few months I've taken a long hot shower before coming here, hoping you wouldn't be able to smell the garbage on me. Now I've changed my mind.

When I started loading garbage, I'd come home every day and stand in the shower for twenty minutes, soaping up and shampooing, trying to get the smell out. I checked myself after I'd dried off, smelling my arm and blowing into my cupped hands. I smelled something. I wasn't sure.

Out on my route, too. After I dumped a can of garbage into the hopper, I'd put my nose right up to my arm and sniff. There, I'd think, that's me. I'm a garbage man. Everyone knows it, just like they knew it about Dad. If they forget, all they've got to do is get near me. They'll smell the rotten vegetables they threw out last night.

I had a girlfriend for a little while. She moved in with us when I was between the two jobs. Her name was Melody and she was sweet and understanding. I didn't deserve her. When I took the sanitation job, I couldn't tell her right away. It hurt too much. But she figured it out. From Mom, maybe. Maybe from the smell.

One day I asked her how she liked the way I smell.

I don't mind it, she said. It just smells like you've been chopping bell peppers.

I had to kick her out. I couldn't stand that she smelled me. She might have smelled bell peppers all right. But someone else had chopped them.

I hated myself, and I tried to make it worse. All day long at work, I'd hold my arm up to my nose and smell it. I'd smell my work shirt, too, and my trousers. Before I emptied the garbage into the hopper, I'd stick my nose into it and take a big whiff. It made me feel good to hate myself. Smell that, I said to myself. Nothing changes. It's the smell you're going to smell all your life.

I started to bring a flask to work. I thought if I drank

enough by afternoon, I'd forget to stick my nose in the garbage and I wouldn't hate myself so much. Sometimes it worked. Then one day I stopped in to see you on my way to work. I'd never done that in the morning before. That day I just sat there and looked at you from across the room for a minute and that was it. I didn't say a word to you. But when I got to work I still had that hospital smell with me, and it reminded me of those balloons I'd blown up as a kid.

I didn't think much of it until I got out on my route. Then I took a big whiff of that first garbage pail, and this time it didn't smell like garbage. It smelled like rotten vegetables, sour milk, grass clippings, wet newspapers, shampoo bottles, diapers, even plastic bags and cardboard boxes. But not garbage. That one smell had become all those separate smells. I smelled every can I emptied that day and none of them smelled like garbage. They smelled like whatever was put in there—bell peppers or potato skins or splintered wood. Every can had something different in it. Some cans had almost the same smells in them. But none were exactly the same.

After that, I began to pay attention to all the individual smells. I stuck my nose in the garbage like before, only now it wasn't for self-pity. Now I wanted to pick out all the smells. I wanted to know what was in there by its smell. I got good at doing it, too. The other loaders saw me and started testing me. They'd have me close my eyes, and they'd put a piece of garbage up to my nose. Once they held up a dead gerbil. Once a carton of rotten eggs. I didn't mind. Almost always, I could tell what it was by the smell. I'd get worried when I couldn't. Sometimes there was no wind and I'd be smelling the same thing all day. That can dull your nose. It's all becoming one smell again, I'd think. Then the wind would pick up and I'd be okay.

That's how I got good at smelling. I can smell just about anything. I can smell the difference between royal palms and coconut palms, between sea grapes and sea oats. I can smell what kind of animal is hiding in the bushes. I can smell a woman's perfume from half a mile away. When there's a breeze coming in off the ocean, I can smell what kind of fish are running offshore. Let me tell you, I can smell. And the important thing about smelling is to pay attention to the wind.

Here's what I've found out, Louis. The wind is talking to us all the time. Most people don't listen, though, because they don't know how to smell. But smelling is the only way to understand the wind. That's how it talks. The wind doesn't make its own smell. It carries the smells of everything else. It might take the smell of a pine tree's sap and carry it down the street to an old man sitting on the porch of a nursing home, looking out at traffic. Then that old man smells that pine sap and remembers when he was a kid and used to chase lizards and squirrels up those pine trees, and after, when he'd hop down and look at his hands, and they'd be covered with sap and little pieces of bark stuck to the sap, like he'd grown a new skin. He'd think, Mama's gonna be mad at me because that ain't never gonna wash off. But now he looks at his old, trembling hands and he sees that it has washed off. He leans back in his chair and smells the sap, remembering what it felt like on his hands, remembering until the smell fades because the wind has taken it somewhere else.

A boy might be walking home one night and he's mad at himself because he lost all his money shooting pool. He's had a few drinks so he's looking at his feet to make sure they move the way he expects them to, and then he smells something, stops, and looks up. He sees that he's in front of his girlfriend's house. He has smelled what he smells when her mother opens the door for him, her mother's housedress that smells a little like floor wax, all the little knickknacks her mother collects that smell like they sat in the Salvation Army store for a year before she bought them, the paint on the mantel that's just beginning to chip. And from all the smells of the house he finds the ones he knows belong only to his girlfriend. The cup of her palms, the inside of her forearm, the shoulder scar from her vaccination, the curls in her hair, and most of all her breath. He reaches out for these smells especially, and he grabs onto them and holds them for as long as he can. Standing before her house he smells all this and he is happy. The wind has brought these smells to him. It is speaking to him. He is just drunk enough that he might go up and rap on her window.

When these things happen, you might start to wonder if the wind is good or evil. But the wind doesn't care one way or another. It talks, and it wants us to listen. And the more we listen, the more it will talk. Not everything it tells us is good, but it's always something we ought to hear.

The only time we should be scared is when the wind stops talking. When the wind is quiet nothing changes. The sky stays the same. The earth stays the same. People stay the same. They smell the same. They smell just like their fathers. When the wind is still, a man can swing a golf club and the ball will go exactly where it is aimed. A man can raise a gun and his hand won't blow to one side or the other. He can fire the gun and the bullet will go exactly where the gun is pointed. Nothing will change its direction. The time between makes no difference. It doesn't count. Nothing will change what happens.

When people want to hurt each other, they throw things at each other—rocks, spears, golf balls, bullets. You take aim and then you let your rock fly, hoping your aim is exact and the rock will hit the other guy's forehead exactly between the eyes, knocking him out, making the blood roll down into his eyes so he can't get up and do the same to you. So the rock gets thrown and everything's looking good. But when things are in the air they belong to the wind, and the wind doesn't work on calculations. The wind likes to blow things around, mess things up, throw off your calculations. It sees a tree full of leaves and decides the leaves are in its way so it blows them all off the tree. Then it sees somebody's piled up the leaves and it decides to mess up the pile. It sees a quarterback put the football up and decides to blow it over to the defensive back. The wind can stop people from hurting each other, too. The wind might see the rock heading for the guy's forehead and decide to blow it off course. Then it just glances off the side of the guy's head. The guy gets mad and throws a rock back at you, but that rock misses completely. Because of the wind. You end up shaking hands with the guy, and you both say, Forget it, we aren't good enough rock throwers to make it worth our time. But really it's the wind. It's not that the wind is trying to teach anybody a lesson. The wind doesn't care about that. It doesn't care about anything. It just likes to push things around. And that's a good thing for us. If there weren't any wind, there'd be a lot more people hurting each other every day. There'd be nothing to throw off their calculations. Golf balls would never miss. Bullets would never miss.

These are the things I've learned about the wind. It changes the direction a bird flies. It changes the look of the sky by blowing the clouds around. It changes the look of the earth, too—sometimes it carries leaves off of plants, and sometimes it carries their seeds and makes them grow somewhere else.

And the wind changes people, too. It carries smells to them and makes them think about things. It talks to people that way. It reminds them that things can change, that things will always change.

That's why I'm here, Louis.

Before I came in, I asked the doctor, Can he smell anything? He didn't know who I was talking about at first. He'd forgotten about you. I reminded him, and I asked him again. Can he smell anything? He said he wasn't sure. He said maybe. I said thank you.

Then I came here to tell you all this. Maybe you haven't heard a word I've said. Maybe you can only hear the sound of the rain and the sound of the gun. But the doctor said maybe you can smell, and if you can smell then the wind can talk to you even if I can't. The wind changes things. The wind can stop the rain. It can blow it away. Then people will come out of their houses again and pick up where they left off. And you can smell the people and what's in their houses, and the trees and plants around their houses, and even the garbage they put out in front of their houses and the garbage men who come to pick it up.

I'm going to try to show you what I mean. I'm going over to the window and I'm going to open it up. I never opened it before because I didn't think it would matter. I didn't think it could change anything. But there are trees out there, Louis. Oak trees and pine trees. There are birds flying between the trees. Blue jays and sparrows. There are squirrels, too, and the squirrels are running in the grass. There are mushrooms in the grass. And blue and yellow wildflowers. There's a parking lot next to the grass, and there are cars pulling in and out of the parking lot. There are people walking to and from their cars, and those people have all sorts of smells—their skin and their clothes and their sweat and their deodorant and shampoo and everything they've had for breakfast and lunch today. I'm going to open the window and you're going to smell them all. The wind is going to bring them to you. Then maybe the rain is going to stop for both of us. Then maybe things will change.

Song for the Deaf

When Tony Sutter gave his first solo performance in fourth grade music class, his chattering classmates shut up and his music teacher's fingertips froze on the ivories. Up and down the hall of Ermine Elementary, the other teachers lost their places in mid-lesson monologues and their students quit strategizing about how to improve their positions in the lunchroom line, while outside, the playground lady, who had just put her lips to her state police enforcement whistle to break up a kickball fight, collapsed on the four-square court and died.

Only Jeremy Jones, standing on the far side of the diamond, passed over by the kickball elect for the twenty-third day in a row, witnessed the playground lady's tragedy—the surprised look behind her granny glasses, her hands clutching her throat, her final slow-motion collapse onto the court. He darted through a tableau of slack-jawed classmates to reach her.

As he knelt beside her, her crow's feet unfurled and her thin lips bloomed to a youthful fullness, and he saw her as if for the first time.

Jeremy Jones had never caused her grief—never cursed or fought or pulled a girl's hair at recess—but neither had he paid her any attention before this. And now it was too late. He was no better than the others.

A shimmer of reflected light drew his eyes to the whistle resting on her chest. She must have bought ever bigger and louder whistles over the years, believing each time the new one would make a difference. He couldn't recall the sound of a single one.

A shiver passed through him. He swallowed once and curled his trembling fingers under the playground lady's head, slid the whistle's cord past her crinkly gray hair. He jumped to his feet and ran.

Only later, as he buffed the whistle's stainless steel skin with the front of his blousy t-shirt, did he discover the metal pea inside was missing. Had the playground lady sucked down the pea when she'd heard Tony Sutter's golden voice? Had she choked to death on it? Or had she stood there blowing and blowing a defective silent whistle until her heart and lungs seized from the effort?

He preferred to think she'd died trying.

•

Jeremy kept the whistle in his pocket every day throughout elementary school, and when he had no pockets—when his ex-hippie single mother dressed him up in sissified pocketless shorts and then, in junior high, when he had to face the pubescent horror of showering in front of his classmates—he gripped the relic tightly in his fist. Sometimes at night, he took it out of his pajama pocket and put it to his lips, knowing the unjust fate of the only other person to do so. He blew. But without the pea, the noise was breathy and weak. If only it had worked for the playground lady, he thought, the pure, authoritative sound of it would have distracted the kids and teachers from Tony Sutter's magnificent voice. Then Tony Sutter might have lived the rest of his life as the stuck-up loser he really was.

Instead, after his glorious day of school-wide acclaim, Tony Sutter began to hold himself in the highest esteem, and for some terrible reason nearly everyone else went along. He changed his name to Antonio—just Antonio—a name he decided fit better with his angelic singing voice. Even his parents had trouble with it at first. They'd been calling him Tony for nine years, so if they slipped up they were to be forgiven—by God, maybe, but not by Antonio, who'd already perfected his tantrum-throwing by studying the backstage antics of moody opera singers in *Opera Talk!* magazine. He stamped his tiny feet and snapped his LPs over his knee until his parents apologized and promised to pronounce "Antonio" with the correct Italian inflection three times over.

"Say it! Say it! Say it!" he yelled, driving his little fist into his soft palm, and they complied as well as they could but never well enough. They were the fifth generation owners of a small ranch, and they'd never met a full-blooded Italian. They'd only heard the accent once years ago, when they'd seen an Italian maitre d' in a movie smack his rounded lips to snap the waiters to attention. But he may have been French, they weren't sure.

"Ain-toh-nee-yo," they said, but stopped short of popping their *oh*-ed lips.

It was okay by them that their son would never take the reins of the family ranch. In fact, everything Antonio did or didn't do was delightful to his devoted parents; he was their golden-haired, angel-voiced baby boy, pure of heart even if his voice killed a hundred playground ladies.

By age eleven, Antonio had let his golden hair grow out. By thirteen, he'd dyed it black. He was old enough then to be regarded as a town misfit, and he wore the mantle proudly—along with the black cape he'd mail-ordered from the opera surplus store. When he walked into town from his family's ranch, his black hair and cape raking behind him like an airy, dual-action farm implement, the other ranchers stopped their work and stared. Antonio's chin was too high, his posture unspeakably perfect. The ranchers leaned over the fence, put a boot up on the lower rail. They nudged each other and laughed.

And the shopkeepers in town didn't like him lingering in their stores. Come back for Halloween, they said. We'll have candy for you then.

In school, the kids used him as a litmus test for witches: touch his hair, and if the dye came off in your hand you were cursed. Bullies yanked at his cape, shouted obscenities in his ear, and tried to kink his perfect posture with well-placed shoves to the spine.

And Antonio didn't care, a maddening fact that made Jeremy Jones squeeze his fist so tight the playground lady's whistle imprinted itself on his palm. Tony had his voice, and everyone, even the bullies, stood in awe of that. The voice turned them so cowed and reverent that when the bullies threw a punch, they threw it considerately, so as not to hit him in the voice box. They blackened his eyes and bent him double with blows to the gut, but to Antonio the black eyes were just a little stage make-up, and a blow to the gut gave him the opportunity to practice his deep bow. The one bully who grazed his throat with a punch, just barely and of course accidentally, bore the wrath of the entire school and got his face scrubbed with a gravy-soaked slab of Salisbury steak.

So when the time came for Antonio's final junior-high recital, the bullies attended, just like nearly everyone else in

Ermine, including the ranchers who laughed at his freakish looks, the shopkeepers who hurried him out of their stores, and Jeremy Jones, whose mother had a compulsive appreciation for the arts and insisted he go.

When Antonio took the stage that night for the finale, all motion stopped, and the entire school auditorium held its breath. He didn't disappoint. His oversized, somewhat rubbery mouth fired piercing volleys of *bel canto* ballistics, and each grateful casualty clutched his heart as if it were Antonio's only target. The Erminers' eyes fell shut and they forgot themselves and their cows and goats and pigs and new boots. They stopped creaking in their fold-down aluminum chairs. They stopped plinking tobacco juice into rusty Del Monte cans. And the incidental noises that usually ran through their heads on a continuous loop—the voices of conscience and desire, the radio weather forecaster's droning report, the lowing and bleats of their animals, the theme songs of their TV shows, the rattles of their aging and overworked machinery, the complaints of their spouses and children—all suddenly shut themselves off, and then they imagined themselves riding through the valley and up into the mountains on Antonio's voice, flying weightless and in love and as pure of heart as the Dead.

Jeremy sat in the back with his arms crossed and a John Deere cap pulled down over his watery eyes, trying not to enjoy himself. But when he looked at the others he saw a glimmer of what he felt in himself, and that scared him. He remembered the playground lady, how she'd choked on that voice and died.

Why couldn't this Tony Sutter just look in the mirror and see himself for the loser he was? His blond eyebrows and jet-black hair made his face look ghoulish. And even the long hair couldn't hide his droopy earlobes. He had a weak chin, a girlish neck, and a thin body with long arms and floppy clown feet. He wasn't tall enough to be charmingly gawky, not small enough to be cute. By all rights, Tony Sutter should have been the bottom-feeder in the social aquarium, the one who slurps the filth off the stem of the plastic plant and the deep sea diver's shoes. But there was that voice, and the voice had saved him. It had lifted him up just enough to leave Jeremy Jones alone at the bottom, forever pressing that useless pea-less whistle to his straining lips.

While Jeremy wasn't as ugly as Tony Sutter, he had an almost unspeakable plainness to him. He was beneath detection even by the bullies, who prided themselves at outing even the subtlest losers and freaks. The most interesting thing about Jeremy was his mother, the town's only remaining ex-hippie, who scraped by selling organic fruit and vegetables at prices just low enough to make her feel she was doing a little good in the world but also suffering for all the good she'd intended to do and hadn't. Unfortunately for Jeremy, the low prices at her fruit and vegetable stand had earned her the town's grudging respect—and that made her less interesting. And she didn't dress or act like a hippie anymore, so she wasn't a source of gossip.

As the junior high recital neared its close, the now *Magnificent Antonio* reaching new heights with each song, Jeremy raised the bill of his cap, desperate for some sign that Tony Sutter's spell could be broken. There were all the bovine faces, eyes closed, eyebrows arched, some of their heads trembling just slightly on their necks like sprung jacks-in-the-box in a breeze, their hands on their knees, or else folded over their chests as though holding their spirits to their bodies, barely. All of them disciples of Tony Sutter.

Except one. Across the aisle, in the back row like Jeremy, she sat between her parents, straight blond hair dangling over the aluminum seat-back, hands in her lap, polite and attentive, but hardly bewitched. In fact, she was struggling against boredom. He could see it in her eyes. He remembered, then: She was deaf.

Jeremy didn't know her name, only that she was never seen far from her parents, the new owners of the Hats and Boots Mart. They schooled her at home, in the apartment above their store downtown. He'd seen her sweeping the store's entry on his way to school sometimes, but this was the first time he'd gotten a good look at her face—small nose and tall forehead, little bulb of a chin, high cheekbones. From a certain angle under these lights, she was as laser-cut as a model, but when she turned her head slightly, the other half of her face folded up the promise of her perfect profile and her looks were plain, underachieving, maybe just underformed.

Jeremy had never gone to church because his mother was agnostic by default, but something about the cathedral ceiling, the enraptured crowd, and—he couldn't deny it—Tony Sutter's angelic voice made him feel a rare sense of mystery, and so he thanked God for making the deaf girl deaf.

As the Magnificent Antonio hit his final notes, each more beautiful than the last, Jeremy thought he heard a new edge in the voice, a fierceness that cut through all that dreamy sweetness. Tony Sutter's face showed increasing annoyance. Not his mouth, which held shape to buff each note that left his golden diaphragm. But his eyes and his furrowed brow. He was staring now at the shopkeeper's daughter and singing only for her, struggling to bring her into his fold. He didn't know she couldn't hear.

Meanwhile, the deaf girl was composed, polite, and totally unaffected. That had to sting Tony Sutter more than any bully's punch.

Jeremy bent over and put his hand to his mouth. As laughter filled his cheeks and sawed out his nose, he missed Antonio's stunning climax.

Later that night, in the dark of his room, Jeremy got down on his knees and rested his forearms on his bedspread. He unclasped his palms and brought the empty whistle to his trembling lips. He sighed into it, the weak rush like a breathy prayer to the God of the Unnoticed.

And so it went, the next night and the next. While Antonio rode the magic carpet of his wondrous voice, Jeremy Jones clung to its fringe with a card up his sleeve and only the faintest hope of ever playing it.

·

In high school, Jeremy slid like a frozen fish off the stainless steel prep counter of teen society. Party invitations floated over his head and behind his back and sometimes, it seemed, right through him. Girls brushed past him in the hall and never broke the flow of their conversations, never even lowered their voices.

Then, when Jeremy was sixteen, his mother founded a local chapter of the Arts Appreciation League and made it her first order of business to take up a collection to send Antonio to a prestigious music school in New York.

The townspeople were eager to give by this time, not so much as art patrons but as people who wanted some peace and quiet. Antonio's endless singing carried throughout the valley and rebounded off the surrounding mountains—causing avalanches, some said. People heard him on their ranches, in their shops and restaurants, even in their showers—the one place where they'd once thought it safe to hum a few bars themselves. They had business to attend to, lives to lead; they couldn't just close their eyes and drift off into the clouds all day. Also, Antonio had grown stranger in his ways. He wore the same old tuxedo every day. The too-wide jacket shifted back and forth like a bell as he walked. His short-legged, wide-waisted pants snapped like flags in a stiff wind. At any moment he might drop to one knee and burst into song, gesturing melodramatically with his small but expressive hands. When he returned to his feet with his trousers drooped low in back, he'd hike them up and hold them with one hand, still gesturing with the other. He'd begun to wear dark make-up around his eyes, and people called him The Singing Dracula.

When the scholarship check was presented to him, the league's co-vice-president patted him on the back. "I just know we'll all be tuning in to PBS real soon to see you whoop the pants off them three tenors."

Antonio accepted the check and the challenge in the name of all artists everywhere, most specifically himself. He bowed deeply, his black hair flopping over his head and sweeping the wood floor of the library meeting room.

The four other people in the room applauded: all three members of the Arts Appreciation League and Jeremy, whose mother had laid her usual guilt trip on him until he agreed to come. He'd had to suffer through dozens of Tony Sutter recitals, Tony Sutter school assemblies, Tony Sutter special achievement awards broadcast over the school intercom. At least this would be the last.

In the library conference room, the clapping went on for an uncomfortably long time, as if they were waiting for a signal from Antonio to end their applause. Antonio, who had no such signal in his otherwise impressive vocabulary of dramatic gestures, never once looked any of them in the eye.

Finally, the librarian reached in and pulled the door shut, squinting her eyes to show mild annoyance.

·

Jeremy soon discovered he hadn't gotten rid of Tony Sutter after all. The Magnificent Antonio wrote long letters home to his parents, who posted them on the city hall bulletin board. Even if Jeremy could have resisted the temptation to read the letters himself, he would have heard them all over town on the lips of others. People seemed to live and die by Antonio's ups and downs, often allowing themselves to be overtaken by the drama of the moment, even when they knew things would turn out all right in the end. They were so certain of it that, even at the time, they referred to this period as the Years of Struggle and found each of Antonio's failures strangely reassuring. Jeremy saw the myth rising up, and like the others, he sometimes found himself believing. He felt powerless.

Antonio's letters related his New York struggles ad nauseam and with surprising candor. In the mountains, he reminded his parents, his voice had resonated perfectly in the bowl-shaped valley; in the city, the narrow concrete canyons thinned out its fierceness, while the car horns and bus brakes smothered its distinctive timbre. Failing all his classes, he soon dropped out of music school.

Only his own unflappable sense of self-importance kept him in New York. He picked up odd jobs around Lincoln Center, worked his way from the loading dock of the Met, inside to the café, and finally backstage, where he toiled as a stagehand's understudy, moving sets around but only in rehearsals or when his man was sick. He sang as he worked, much to the annoyance of the others. To them, he was beyond aloof; he swam through life in an ego-massaging hot tub of self-praise. Almost universally shunned, his prospects steadily dimmed until the season they performed Wagner's *Ring*. The craggy set of *Die Walküre* brought out the qualities in Antonio's voice that hadn't been heard since the mountains. The director noticed, and when both a singer and his understudy shared stale knish and got food poisoning, Antonio was tapped to play one of the bloodthirsty hounds who chase Siegmund and Sieglinde, a role unique to this production.

The Magnificent Antonio finally took the stage, chin perhaps not as high and vertebrae not aligned quite as neatly as they'd been a couple of years earlier, owing to the hard times and hard work. A drop of sweat found its way through his make-up and trickled down his snout. When at last the moment came to bark out his lines, his *vuf-vufs* and rolling-r-*grrrs*, he balked.

According to the letter he scrawled at the bus station and which arrived home just before he did, Antonio felt a sharp pang of guilt up on stage for the way he'd treated the folk back home. He'd deprived them of his perfect voice and abandoned them to *the unlovely clatter of the everyday* (those words scrolled across his brain that night like a subtitle translation in his ongoing personal opera). And then, he wrote, a tear formed at the corner of his eye, right there in front of all the cosmopolitan operagoers and the incestuous twins he was chasing across the stage. He broke character, strode through the fog of the mountainous set, and yelled out at the stunned audience through his furry snout: "My voice belongs to the people!"

When he bowed, his dyed black hair fell loose and cleared a space in the fog.

•

Like everyone else, Jeremy Jones read the letter on the city hall bulletin board. He, for one, had never minded *the unlovely clatter of the everyday.* During Antonio's years in New York, Jeremy had escaped high school with a diploma and gone on to police academy. His mother sobbed at his graduation, partly because she'd never imagined she'd have a cop for a son, but mostly because she'd secretly been dating the town's sheriff, indulging in the guilty pleasure of whispering his name in motel rooms and the back of his squad car, growling the *r* of his last name—Grrreeley—just slightly for effect. She worried that her son knew all about her affair and had turned cop either to spite her or to act out his unresolved Oedipal fantasies.

She was wrong: Jeremy knew nothing about it, not yet. And he suspected nothing when Sheriff Greeley hired him as his deputy, even though the town had never had one before.

Like almost everything else in Ermine, the crime was second rate. Every so often, there'd be a fight to break up, a drunk and disorderly to drive home, a borrowed tool not returned on time. But the fight was usually between the same pair of chubby girls in the trailer park who screamed a lot better than they scratched, the drunk and disorderly usually tipped him for the ride, and the borrowed tool was broken anyway. Few people outside the city government even realized that Ermine had a police force, and those who did figured that being a police officer in Ermine was the next best thing to not being one.

And then the Magnificent Antonio returned. Jeremy got wind of it and made a point of sipping coffee at the Trailways Station/American Legion Hall when the bus came in.

"Ain-TOH-nee-yo!" the Sutters said when they met their son at the back door of the station, holding their lips in the shape of an *o*.

Jeremy had struggled his whole life just to feel part of the unlovely clatter Tony Sutter so loftily dismissed. With the Magnificent Antonio back in Ermine, he again felt cast out. But with his hand on the pocket of his police uniform, where he kept his pea-less whistle, he reminded himself that now, at least, he was in a position of some authority. He had only to wait for an opportunity to use it.

Hopeful again, he touched his lips to his mug of hot coffee and blew a kind of prayer: *whew.*

•

At first, Antonio's voice was welcomed back to the valley. He sang on the streets of the town and in the stores when he ran errands for his parents, and during weekly recitals at the school auditorium, sponsored by the Arts Appreciation League, Jeremy Jones' mother still serving an indefinite term as president.

At his card table desk in the corner of city hall, Jeremy seemed to work at the exact point of resonance for Tony Sutter's voice. After days of torture, he ventured a rare suggestion to Sheriff Greeley, who was watching a western with his feet up on the mayor's rolltop, his usual position when he wasn't out on mysteriously long patrols in the town's only police car.

"Does that qualify as disturbing the peace?"

The sheriff kept his eyes on *Rio Bravo.* "What's that?"

"The singing."

"Mm. Pretty, ain't it?"

Jeremy put a hand to his belt and asked permission to use the bathroom.

After a week or two, most of the town reacted to Antonio's voice the way the sheriff did. Their lives spun like tractor wheels in the mud, full of *unlovely clatter*, and Antonio's voice had become just another track in the continuous loop.

Antonio seemed to sense his diminishing powers to startle and amaze, and something happened that even New York hadn't done to him: his unflappable sense of self-importance began flapping. His posture slumped and his blond roots showed and just maybe his voice wasn't quite as lovely. He was on a downward spiral, but only Jeremy Jones saw it happening; his constant irritation had the undesirable effect of making him too-aware of Tony Sutter's every expression, and the look on Tony's face these days reminded Jeremy of that moment long ago at the junior high recital when the Magnificent Antonio was tormented by the deaf girl.

So maybe it was fate after all that led Antonio through the door of the Hats and Boots Mart one afternoon. In popular memory, Antonio arrives there on an errand to buy new boots for his mother's birthday. In the diary of a local gas station attendant, Antonio was singing his way through town when a mannequin's cape caught his eye in the window display. The editor of the *Ermine Mountain Tribune-Gazette and Auto/ Truck Flyer* maintains that Antonio intentionally sought the challenge of the deaf girl, as he was singing what sounded like an Italian version of "Careless Love." Nearly everyone now believes there were larger forces at work.

As Antonio waited for the owner to dig up some plus-size boots for his mother (or to pull the cape off the mannequin), he sang a German aria he'd learned in the city (or the Italian "Careless Love"). Something caught his eye, and he turned to the deaf girl sweeping the floor. He didn't seem to connect her then with that bored face at his junior high recital. Maybe he never did. He only admired her perfect posture and the way her straight blond hair fell over her shoulders and curled inward no matter how many times she flipped it back. He liked the peasant-girl dress she wore, which fit neatly with his now-famous decision to sing for "the people," whom he imagined as European peasants with caps and dirty vests and noble but obsolete jobs.

Still singing, Antonio paid the girl's father then pulled open the glass door. At that precise moment, it's now believed, he glanced back at the deaf girl, and seeing her at exactly the right angle to accentuate her best features, he fell in love.

Jeremy saw the whole thing out on foot patrol. As deputy, he'd made it his habit to pass by the Hats and Boots Mart when he knew the deaf girl would be doing her chores. He'd never forgotten the effect her deafness and her mercurial face had had at the junior high recital, and he tried now and then to sneak a look at her, to decide once and for all if she was pretty or not, and whether that mattered or not. This time, he saw only the look on Tony Sutter's definitely butt-ugly face, and he was certain Tony Sutter was doomed.

Because what did the angel-voiced Tony Sutter have to offer a deaf girl? Nothing at all. Or, put another way, exactly as much as Jeremy Jones.

•

According to witnesses, Antonio's serenade began a few minutes after ten on a clear but moonless Wednesday night. A second-story light came on above the Hats and Boots Mart when his first sonic volley broke the calm. He paced back and forth under the girl's dark window, singing and gesturing as if carrying on a melodramatic debate with himself. By now he'd heard the girl was deaf, and he was convinced that his voice would soon transcend that minor obstacle. After all, who better than she could appreciate both the unworldly perfection of his voice and the fearful depth of feeling behind it? Her mind was absolutely uncluttered by *the unlovely clatter of the everyday*. She wasn't looking for momentary escape. His voice, when she heard it, would be the only thing she heard, the only thing she'd ever heard. She might not hear a sound exactly, but something purer and utterly uncompromised.

When the townspeople heard him, they peeled back their curtains and pulled up their blinds, and some of them said aloud, "Mm, pretty," not speaking to anyone but saying it because they thought it needed to be said. After a few minutes of silent appreciation, they turned back to their radios, TVs, and orthopedic pillows, hoping the pretty noise would again fade into the background.

But Antonio sang louder. He lowered himself to one knee and put his hand to his heart. He held the high notes until his neck trembled and the windows of the Hats and Boots Mart shuddered in their frames. All the windows in town were lit but that of his beloved.

The girl's father called the police, after first calling to see if there were police. Of course both sheriff and deputy had heard the singing the moment it began. The sheriff had been watching *Viva Zapata!* with his feet up on the mayor's rolltop when he turned down the sound. "Mm. Pretty," he said, and Jeremy, sitting at his card table stacked high with decades of incomplete paperwork, cringed. His new earplugs weren't working.

"Come on," said the sheriff when he'd hung up the phone. He tucked the front of his flannel shirt into his jeans.

They got into the old Dodge patrol car and drove the two blocks because the sheriff didn't care for walking.

"Just leave this to me," said the sheriff, "but watch carefully. One day soon you'll need to handle these things yourself."

Too distracted at the prospect of locking up Tony Sutter, Jeremy didn't bother to ask what he meant. His best opportunity was finally at hand.

The lights were on up and down the town's main street—in the apartments above the grocery store and the gas station/hunting supplies shop, and in the trailer park wedged between them. Increasingly annoyed faces peered out the windows and the cherubic fighting girls in the trailer park began to shove each other. The peace was getting disturbed.

Antonio sang as though he'd been given a second chance at stardom. This time, he was standing, he knew, at the exact location on earth best suited to his voice.

When the sheriff stopped his car and shut off the motor, Jeremy had his hand on the door handle. The sheriff paused for a moment, as if enjoying the sound, then at last he took a breath and stepped out of the car. Jeremy followed.

"Son!" the sheriff shouted at Antonio. He strode over and dropped his big hand onto Antonio's bony, cape-covered shoulder. The golden voice didn't waver.

"Son! I ain't gonna ask what you been drinking or smoking. I'm just gonna *insist* you step into the squad car."

When Antonio didn't respond, the sheriff fumbled behind him. He'd forgotten the cuffs, but Jeremy was right there with his own, scoring an assist. The sheriff snapped them onto one of Antonio's wrists, and he was reaching for the other when he got a call on his cell phone. He could have quickly completed the arrest, but the sheriff was then the only one in town with a cell phone, and in Ermine there were only a few narrow shafts of unobstructed reception, so he flinched in amazement when it buzzed. He took the call, still holding Antonio's arm with one hand, leaving the cuff to dangle from Antonio's wrist.

All Jeremy could think about was the open dangling cuff. How easy it would be to grab Tony's other wrist, twist it behind his back, and clamp it closed.

"I know it's beautiful, darlin', but the whole town wants him put away," the sheriff was saying into the phone. "There's a motion down at city hall to declare these The Nuisance Years. People're getting tired of waiting for the Glory Years."

Antonio's free hand lifted and fondled each Italian syllable that left his lips. The window above remained dark. The other second-story window had filled with the girl's father, hands on hips, undershirt half-tucked into his pajama bottoms, belly pressed against the windowpane, the model of a peasant patriarch.

The townspeople had begun to open their windows and make unlovely noises. They'd turned up their TVs and radios and still couldn't hear their shows. Some of them were trying to sleep. Some of them had to work for a living, goddamnit. And the chubby girls had begun to pull each other's hair.

The voice was so strong and full of yearning, the notes so purely sung, Jeremy began to think Tony might pull it off after all, and soon. He wondered about the deaf girl in bed. Was she stirring? Was she tucking her straight blond hair behind one ear because she thought she heard something? Were her smallish red lips parting in growing astonishment?

Jeremy stepped closer and put himself into position. All he

had to do was to snap out at that lifted, vibrato wrist and yank it down and he'd be rid of Tony Sutter for good.

"Sure thing, darlin'," said the sheriff. He gave Jeremy a sharp pinch on the bicep as he pulled the cell phone away from his ear. He held the phone up over his head, and for a moment they all stood there—Jeremy, the sheriff, and the person on the other end of the line—and listened.

Jeremy clenched his fists, unable to deny the voice's heartfilling beauty. As tears welled up in his eyes, the shouts of the townspeople became operatic sobs, the chubby fighting girls became supernumeraries, and the Hats and Boots Mart became the set of his own riveting drama. He'd devoted his entire youth to his hatred of Tony Sutter, and yet here he was on the verge of giving up, wishing despite himself for the serenade to work, for the deaf girl to curl her fingers around the thin white curtains until the light captured her astonished blue eyes and made the whole town fall in love.

Smiling dreamily, the sheriff put the phone back to his ear. "Here we are, front row at the Paris opera house, just like you always said…"

A window broke nearby—one of the chubby fighting girls had gotten the upper hand.

Jeremy tensed himself. Antonio was coming to the end of a song, and when his wrist fell with the final note, sheriff or no sheriff, Jeremy would cuff him and bend him into the patrol car like he was taught in police academy.

"We could have that for real, darlin'," the sheriff was saying. "All it takes is the courage to tune in and drop out, to paraphrase a little someone I know…"

As Jeremy raised his hand to strike, a big smile broke over the sheriff's face, and he said something Jeremy didn't catch.

He snapped his phone shut and slapped down Jeremy's wrist.

"You keep this situation under control," he said. "But let him sing, by God. For a good twenty minutes. Then you do whatever you like with this godforsaken hole of a town." He unlocked the cuffs and freed Antonio's thin wrist.

Jeremy watched the sheriff, suddenly thirty pounds lighter, trot back to the patrol car, fling himself inside it, and peel down the same dark side street where Jeremy and his mother still shared a house. He'd taken Jeremy's handcuffs with him.

As Antonio began a new song, the chubby girls' fight spilled out of the trailer and into the dirt. Their mother stood in the door yelling at them. Others banged on their walls and windowsills and shouted at Jeremy to just for God's sake *do something. Does this town have a police force? Are you it? Wasn't there another guy there a minute ago? Are you all being paid by the hour?*

Alone with Tony Sutter on the dark street, Jeremy couldn't move.

Some would say he didn't have the courage to shoot out the tires of destiny. But that wasn't it. Something else had come over him. Despite all his prayers for Tony Sutter to suffer, to be stricken so badly it would take him down for good, it was Jeremy who'd fallen in love with the deaf girl. And now each beautiful note out of Antonio's golden throat expressed with almost unbearable precision the yearning Jeremy felt in his chest. He wanted more than anything—even more than he wanted Tony Sutter to be shackled and gagged—for the deaf girl to appear at her window in all her somewhat bland but ethereal beauty.

As he stepped out from behind Tony Sutter and into the cone of the dim streetlight, he reached into his pocket. He and

Antonio stood together now, the one singing, the other just staring up at the dark window with an ache he did not know how to fix.

The tears started down Jeremy's cheeks. In a last-ditch attempt to steady himself, he pulled out the stainless steel relic and raised it to his quivering lips. He blew as hard as he could, the way the playground lady had tried to in grade school long ago.

The townspeople who witnessed it would say now that not even a sheriff's whistle could stop the angelic voice of the Magnificent Antonio. So strong and insistent was his voice that it blotted out whatever shrill unlovely noise Deputy What's His Name had hoped would steal Antonio's thunder. It was a sign, they said. For at that very moment, the deaf girl's light came on and her plain but vaguely pleasing face appeared at the window.

Antonio turned to Jeremy Jones and looked him in the eye for once, smiling in a way that showed how humbled he was by his own great talent. All the doubts about his ultimate destiny flooded out of his eyes and he was once again the Magnificent Antonio, now at the dawn of his Glory Years.

•

After that, nothing could hold Antonio back. He left town, sacrificing whatever true feelings he might have had for the deaf girl, because how could he let himself love just one person when his voice expressed such deep love for all mankind?

The rest of his story is public knowledge. The quick rise to opera stardom, the great performances on the world's stages, and a victory over the three tenors in the PBS special, "Sing-off in Stockholm."

At first it bothered Jeremy that the whole town attributed the deaf girl's awakening to Tony Sutter's voice instead of the miracle of the whistle. But he soon got over it. The only people who counted knew the truth: himself and the deaf girl. Her name was Marietta, and she was impressed that he took signing lessons so he could ask her on a date. After only a few months, during which he was promoted indefinitely to Acting Sheriff when it was clear Sheriff Greeley—and Jeremy's mother—would never return to Ermine, he signed the question to her, and they were married in June.

Sometimes at night, he still takes out the playground lady's whistle and tells Marietta its story in bed, concluding with that moment under her window when he finally ran the Magnificent Antonio out of town for good. He signs the story expertly, adding exaggerated hand flourishes for emphasis.

And she believes it all, affirming always that the whistle is indeed what she'd heard that night. Jeremy smiles, not caring if she's lying—sort of hoping, in fact, that she is, because then it means she's doing it out of love, and love, he's decided, is the Great Consolation he deserves for his years clutching the chain-link fence of Tony Sutter's undeserved fame.

And then, at Marietta's request, he blows the whistle once more, and she puts her hand on his chest and softly closes her fingers to ask him to please dim the lights.

JOHN HENRY FLEMING is the author of *The Legend of the Barefoot Mailman*, a novel, *Fearsome Creatures of Florida*, a literary bestiary, and *The Book I Will Write*, a serial novel-in-emails. His short stories have appeared in journals such as *McSweeney's, the North American Review, Mississippi Review, Fourteen Hills*, and *Carve*, and have been anthologized in *100% Pure Florida Fiction* and in *The Future Dictionary of America*. His awards include a Literature Fellowship from the State of Florida. He has a PhD in Creative Writing from The University of Louisiana-Lafayette, and is the founding editor of *Saw Palm: Florida literature and art*.

ALSO BY JOHN HENRY FLEMING

The Legend of the Barefoot Mailman
Fearsome Creatures of Florida
The Book I Will Write